"That year, a little over six years since meeting Hannah van Harben, life for me was just about as good as it could get." David Conway is happily married with a young daughter, and wants for nothing. He has an idyllic life on the colony world of Chalcedony, with friends Matt and Maddie, Hawk and Kee – but things are about to get interesting when the friends holiday at Tamara Falls on the planet's equatorial plateau. Buried far beneath the Falls is a dormant alien army – the Skeath, ancient enemies of the Yall: an army which is threatening to come to life, if the evil Dr Petronious gets his way... *Starship Spring* is the triumphant conclusion to the *Starship Quartet*.

STARSHIP SPRING

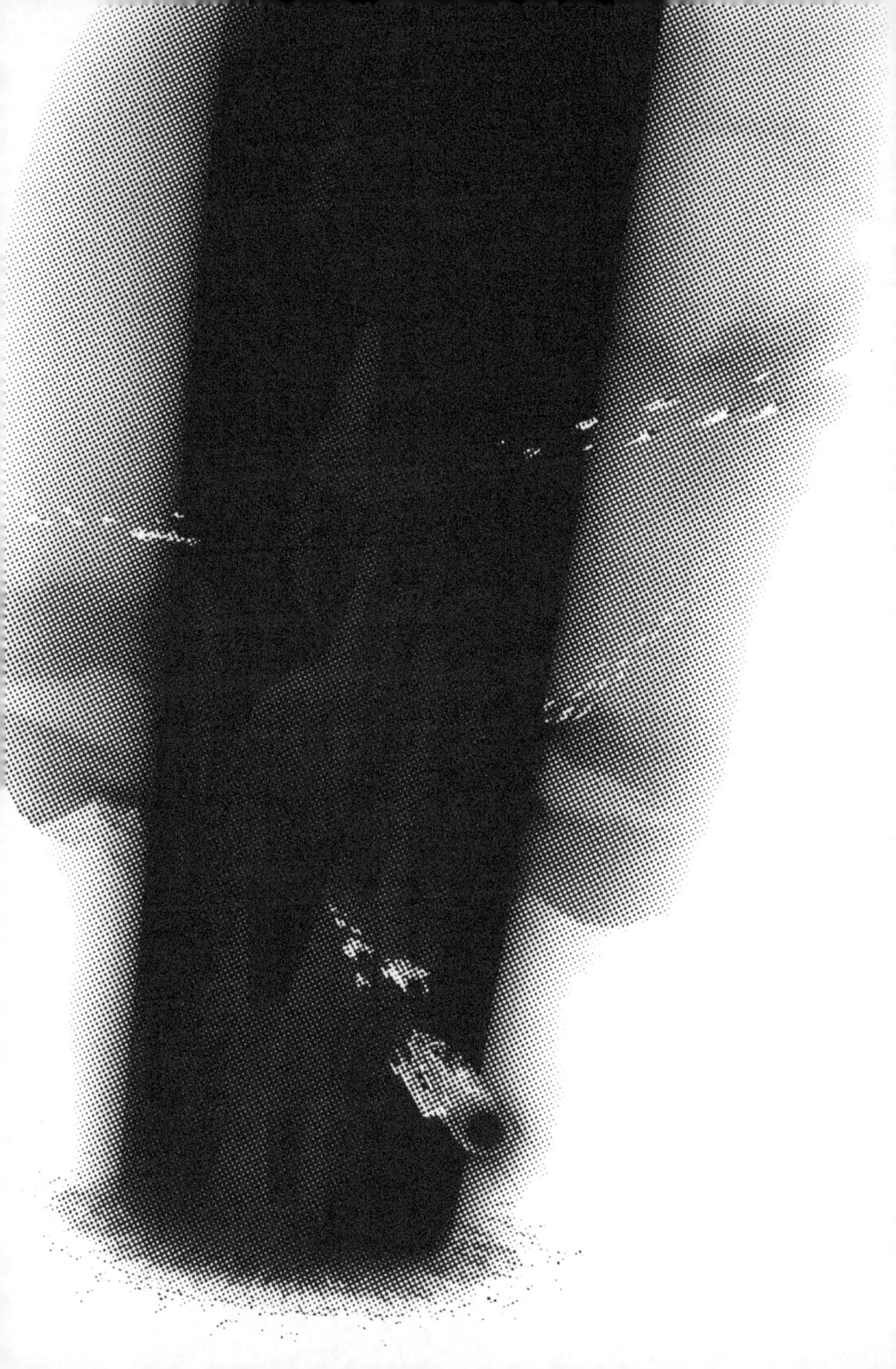

ERIC BROWN
STARSHIP SPRING

Starship Spring
Copyright © 2012 Eric Brown.

The right of Eric Brown to be identified as Author of this Work has been asserted by him in accordance with the Copyright, Designs and Patents Act 1988.

Published in July 2012 by PS Publishing Ltd by arrangement with the author.
All rights reserved by the author.

FIRST EDITION

ISBN
978-1-848634-87-9 (Unsigned edition)
978-1-848634-88-6 (Signed edition)

This book is a work of fiction. Names, characters, places and incidents either are products of the author's imagination or are used fictitiously. Any resemblance to actual events or locales or persons, living or dead, is entirely coincidental.

Jacket art © 2012 Tomislav Tikulin.
Book design by Pedro Marques.
Text set in Sabon.
Titles set in Trajan.

Printed in England by the MPG Books Group
on Vancouver Cream Bookwove 80 gsm stock.

PS Publishing Ltd
Grosvenor House
1 New Road
Hornsea, HU18 1PG
England
E-mail: editor@pspublishing.co.uk
Visit our website at www.pspublishing.co.uk.

STARSHIP SPRING

ONE

AFTER THREE MONTHS OF MILD WINTER, spring comes to Chalcedony in a sudden burst of activity. First the swordbills return *en masse* and take up residence in the shola trees that line the foreshore. Then the shola trees turn from silver to green and send forth their luscious, pendant blooms, and an army of alien insects gives voice to a constant a cappella chirring, welcoming the onset of the warmer weather.

The residents of Magenta Bay, after wintering in the south or on Earth, return home. Shops and cafes open along the waterfront and tourists take advantage of the coast's scenic beauty and bring with them news from around the Expansion.

That year, a little over six years since meeting Hannah van Harben, life for me was just about as good as it could get. It was a long time since anything of any note had occurred to disturb the placid regime of my existence, and that was fine by me.

—

I had not seen my friends for more than six months. Matt and Maddie had been touring the Expansion with Matt's latest artwork; Hawk and Kee had been on a long haul across the galaxy, taking rich tourists on a trip to the Nilakantha stardrift. Normally, the absence of my friends for so long—after enjoying their company almost every day for years—would have sent me into a spiral of loneliness and self-pity. But marriage can be a great corrective to these maladies, and though I missed my friends and our drinking sessions in the Jackeral, family life filled my time, my thoughts and my emotions.

I suspected Hannah was planning something. After six years of marriage I knew her so well that I was picking up subliminal signs: hesitations in conversation, smiles and glances away when I tried to probe.

And then there were the more obvious indicators: com-calls abruptly terminated when I entered the room, then a call that Hannah insisted on taking alone.

For a ludicrous second I entertained the notion that she was having an affair—even though our marriage seemed idyllic—and I think my apprehension made her come clean.

It was four o'clock and the sun was shimmering on the scaled surface of the bay. Hannah had finished work early and we were enjoying a cold beer on the verandah of the *Mantis*.

"Do you miss them?" she asked, watching me closely above her raised glass.

"I do. It's only when they're away that I realise how important they are to me. We've been through a lot together. That said . . ."

"Yes?"

"You and Ella mean more to me than anyone else in the world."

She reached out and gripped my hand, then released it quickly, stood up and made for the lounge. "What?" I said.

She paused in the doorway. "Shhh. Wait there."

Intrigued, I watched swordbills swoop over the distant headland where Matt and Maddie had their dome.

Hannah appeared a minute later, carrying a silver envelope.

"What is it?"

She sat down and tapped the envelope with a long fingernail. "Wouldn't you like to know."

I laughed. "Out with it. What've you been planning?"

She pulled a face. "Was it so obvious?"

"You've been up to something for weeks."

She passed me the envelope, watching me closely, a slight, pursed smile of anticipation gathering her lips.

I unzipped the seal and tipped out the contents: it was one of those gimmicky talking brochures. Activated by my touch, a honeyed feminine contralto purred: "Thank you for selecting a Meredith Summer Break."

I thumbed it into silence and watched a series of idyllic images play themselves out across the surface of the brochure, accompanied by explanatory captions.

"Nestled on the edge Chalcedony's equatorial plateau," I read, "Meredith villas are a series of luxurious holiday retreats . . . "

I gazed at A-frames and silver domes cantilevered over geometrically perfect waterfalls, and free-form extruded glass houses seemingly oozing between hundred-metre-high trees.

I looked up. "But . . . we can't afford this!" I laughed.

"Well, we could, at a push. But we don't have to."

"You're talking in riddles."

She smiled. "Matt can. He contacted me a couple of weeks ago. Some billionaire tycoon bought the ten-year rights to Matt's latest creation. He called to say he wanted to celebrate when he got back."

"So that's what all those calls were about!"

Hannah laughed. "I had to liaise between Matt, Hawk, and the people at Meredith villas. It took some sorting out."

I had never been farther inland than the Yall's Golden Column. The continent's little-explored interior was a mountainous region of vast rainforests, spectacular rivers ten times as long as the Amazon, and abundant alien wildlife.

"We're meeting Matt and Maddie, Hawk and Kee there next week, and staying for a fortnight. Another beer?"

While Hannah fetched a second bottle, I activated the brochure.

"A special feature of your Meredith break," the seductive voice said, "is a one-off and strictly limited tour of the archaeological site at Tamara Falls . . . "

I stilled the image and the voice died. When Hannah returned, I indicated the brochure. "Isn't that where there was that big hush-hush discovery made a few years ago?"

"That's the place, David. And we'll be granted special access."

I whistled. "This must have cost Matt a fortune."

"Typical of the man's generosity," Hannah said. "We have some wonderful friends."

The sound of an approaching ground-car broke the silence. The woman in the driving seat halted before the *Mantis*, waved and called out, "Here she is, on the dot of five as promised. One slightly grubby and very tired little girl."

"Thanks, Lola," Hannah called.

Ella erupted from the rear of the car, a miniature version of Hannah, all long blonde hair and gangly limbs. She sped towards the *Mantis* as the roadster turned and roared away.

Seconds later Ella sprinted through the doorway and launched herself onto my lap. Her weight activated the brochure and the mellifluous woman's voice, muffled under my daughter's bottom, said, "Thrill to the unspoilt splendour of the Tamara Caves, wonder at the natural . . ." I pulled the brochure from under Ella, switched off the sound and passed it to her.

Ella smelled of school, that inimitable perfume of little girl sweat, computer keyboards and memory-dough. She grabbed the brochure. "Starry," she said, the latest superlative she'd picked up from friends. "Tamara Falls!"

"Would you like to go there for a holiday?" Hannah asked.

Ella beamed. "Holiday? Us? Me and you and Daddy?"

Hannah nodded. "And Maddie and Matt, Kee and Hawk."

"Everybody!" Ella trilled. "I haven't seen them for years and years!"

"Well," I said, "perhaps a few months."

She regarded the brochure. "Lizzy says that alien ghosts live in Tamara Falls," she said with all the authority of a five-year-old. "Lizzy told me the ghosts are not very nice. She knows."

I smiled. "Does she now?"

Ella nodded seriously. "She told me. Her Daddy works at Tamara." She leapt off my knee with the sudden, disconcerting transference of attention common to children, and said, "Where's Mr Noodle Pie, Mummy?" And then, "I'm hungry!"

"Noodle Pie's in your room, on the floor where you left him this morning. And there's a samosa in the cooler."

Ella ran off and Hannah took her place on my lap. She kissed my forehead. "Idyllic interior scenery *and* alien ghosts," she said.

I backhanded a tress of golden hair from her cheek. "Can't wait to see Matt and the others, Hannah. Catch up with what they've been doing . . ."

Overhead, a swordbill shrieked a deafening mating call and dived towards the bay.

TWO

THE FIVE DAYS BEFORE we were due to set off inland seemed to drag.

I filled the time with the usual pursuits. I looked after Ella while Hannah was at work in Mackinley, and when Ella was at school I read or took long walks around the bay. In the evenings we had a meal on the verandah, and when Ella went to bed, Hannah and I chatted about her work—she was investigating a rare bank robbery that had occurred in the capital last week—and looked ahead to the holiday.

Ella wanted to know all about Tamara Falls. "Will there be an animal farm?" she asked one day on the way back from school.

"I'm sure there'll be animals near the villa," I temporised.

"And will Hawk and Kee tell me all about the places they've been to in their spaceship?"

I laughed. "Hawk'd like nothing better."

I gripped her small hand as we walked along the foreshore. Ella had been a late and unexpected bonus to a life I had thought complete: after two years of trying for a child, we'd resigned ourselves to having only each other—and although that was fine by me, I was troubled by the fact that Hannah wanted a child. My guilt was expunged one day when she came up to me in the kitchen and said, "You don't have to go to the medical centre for that sperm test, David."

I looked at her. "What, I can do it at home?" I asked, abstractedly.

"Idiot." She mimed a slap across my cheek. "I'm pregnant."

I had thought that life could never be any better, and then Ella came along and showed me what I'd been missing.

Now she pointed a finger towards the *Mantis*. "Tell me the story of the Yall, Daddy."

So for perhaps the hundredth time I told her all about the Yall, the Opening of the Way, and my involvement in it.

On the night before we were due to leave for the interior, we packed cases and gathered together everything we might need for two weeks in the rainforest. The resulting mountain of baggage was sufficient to equip a small army.

We packed Ella off to bed early, because we were setting off just after the crack of dawn, and after a light meal had an early night ourselves.

For some reason I could not get to sleep. I usually slept well and snored like an earth-mover to prove it, as Hannah was always telling me. That night, however, I lay awake for hours, and when I did slip into a light doze, something would wake me and I'd start upright as if from the effects of a nightmare.

Eventually, I slipped out of bed and moved through the ship to the kitchen.

I poured myself a glass of sava juice and stood by a side-screen, staring out at the bay, silvered by the light from the Ring of Tharssos. The damned thing was, I was dead on my feet; my limbs were heavy and I could feel my eyes drooping. I knew I'd suffer for my insomnia when the alarm went off at six and Hannah marshalled us with all the efficiency of a drill sergeant.

I turned to retrace my steps back to bed—and stopped dead in my tracks.

A vaguely familiar figure stood before me in the entrance to the corridor.

It seemed to float, light and ethereal, as I stared. Tall and attenuated, it was more amphibian than mammal, with scales and a pair of gills below its abnormally thin skull: the image of a Yall.

It cast an eerie green glow, the only illumination in the room.

I leaned against the wall for support. "What do you want?"

Perhaps I should have been frightened at the sudden presence of this apparition—frightened not because it betokened some bizarre supernatural phenomenon, but because I guessed that its appearance was the harbinger of imminent crucial events.

After all, the Yall do not show themselves—or their avatars—without due cause, as I knew full well.

I stared at the apparition with an odd calm, a certain fatalism at the fact of its presence.

I said again, "What do you want?"

I did not expect it to answer me verbally: after all, that was not how the first apparition, all those years ago, had communicated with me. Rather, then I had heard its words in my dreams.

So I was more than a little surprised when the elongated alien wraith raised a hand and spoke. "Do not be alarmed."

Suddenly, I wanted Hannah to be with me, to share the experience. I had the intuition that it would be a long time before it might happen again.

"Fine. I'm not alarmed. What do you want?"

"I want," breathed the figure, its voice soft, feathery, "you to show courage in the days that follow."

My heart began a laboured thudding. "Courage?" I parroted stupidly.

"I want you to show the courage, resourcefulness and humanity you showed the very first time you were called upon to do the bidding of the Yall."

I nodded. "What do you want?" I asked for the third time.

"You will be tested, David Conway, you will be tested and found equal to the task."

"What task?"

"You will be guided along the way by others charged with this duty. Be prepared. Do not fear. All will be well."

"I will be tested, along with my friends?" I said.

"Your friends, too, yes."

I nodded that I understood. "What do you want me to do?"

The alien spectre paused before saying, "We want you to follow the dictates of your . . . humanity, David Conway, and all will be well."

Then, before my eyes, the figure began to fade: the corridor behind it gained substance as the spectre became no more than a smoky outline, and then vanished altogether.

I stepped forward. "But what do you want me to do?" I pleaded.

Silence. The ghost was gone. I stood on the threshold of the corridor, my hand outstretched in futile supplication, my heart thudding in the aftermath of the encounter.

I wanted to tell Hannah, but at the same time I didn't want to alarm her.

I returned to bed, lay down beside her and closed my eyes. I reached out, lay a hand on her warm ribcage, felt her solidity, her humanity, and was reassured.

Miraculously, I slept like a babe and woke refreshed before the alarm sounded.

As I showered, I thought back to my audience with the alien ghost, and I honestly did not know whether to feel elation at what its appearance might augur, or apprehension.

—

We took a taxi down the coast to Mackinley, then caught the newly established monotrain, which left the coast and wound through the foothills of the central mountains. For the next hour, as the train bored through the mountain, Ella slept and Hannah buried herself in a detective novel on her flatscreen, harrumphing frequently at the author's technical errors.

I smiled as I watched her and tried not to think of what had occurred last night.

We emerged from the mountain and burst into shocking sunlight. Ahead were the brilliant green swathes of the interior rainforest, and I was reminded that this was not Brazil by the frequent appearance of bizarre alien growths: trees that shot up a hundred metres above the forest canopy and exploded in a riot of bloody, balloon-like blooms; succulent flowers the size of spinnakers on long stalks beside the track. Ella woke up and stared through the window in amazement.

Hannah said in a whisper, "What's wrong, David?"

"Wrong? Why?" I shook my head, unaware that I'd evinced anything other than my usual behaviour.

Her detective's gimlet eyes skewered me. "You've been quiet all morning. And last night you didn't sleep. You were in the kitchen, muttering to yourself."

"I'm fine. I couldn't sleep. I'm still tired." I smiled. "Hell, look at that . . . " I pointed to an ape-analogue perched on the branch of a tree and staring in at us lugubriously, purple-haired and impossibly thin.

An hour later we came to the central plain and stared in wonder at the Golden Column perhaps fifty kilometres distant.

It never fails to affect me like this. I feel a welling up inside, an emotional constriction that seems to be lodged in my chest. I tell myself that I feel this way because of my direct involvement with the Column, but I know that's not wholly true. Everyone feels overcome with a surge of some strange emotion—akin to nostalgia, verging on awe—at the sight of the powerful uprushing of golden light spearing from the land.

The reaction has something to do with its alien provenance, of course, and with what the column can do. Starships enter the column and emerge at a destination entered into their smartcores, whether that destination is within the same solar system or thousands of light years distant. That is miracle enough, but more astounding still is the fact that wherever the starships emerge, they reproduce a Golden Column, effectively establishing gateways through which other ships can pass.

Even as we watched, hundreds of tiny starships moved into and emerged from the column like busy insects. Hannah was staring at the Column with tears in her eyes. She reached out and gripped my hand.

Ella scrambled onto my knee. "Tell me about how you found out about the Golden Column, Daddy!"

Dutifully, I recounted the story once again.

The rest of the journey passed without incident and we arrived at Tamara Falls three hours later.

THREE

TAMARA FALLS WAS A GREAT RIFT in the rainforest on the edge of a plateau two thousand metres above sea level. The gash in the land had scabbed over millennia ago and was now overgrown with emerald rainforest; the only evidence of the rift was the mighty river that poured over the lip of the plateau and fell a thousand metres in a perfect arc. On either side of the escarpment, nestling amid the riot of vegetation that tumbled down the incline, an assortment of villas sparkled in the late afternoon sunlight: traditional domes, A-frames, and the unique diaphanous "retorts" for which the complex was famous, a series of bulbous habitats that flowed and fitted around the trees like a glass-blower's daydream.

The monorail terminated beside a placid lagoon at the foot of the Falls. We disembarked and took a cable car up the incline, the trees so close on either side that you could reach out and caress the foliage. We were the only passengers in the carriage.

We stood by the glass window and watched the lagoon and the tiny station diminish in our wake, the features becoming more tiny and toy-like the higher we climbed.

Ella giggled. "Look at the train! It's like a little worm. How did we fit in it?"

"It's getting smaller because of perspective," Hannah said. "I told you all about perspective last week."

Ella frowned. "Like when Daddy complains about the building in Mackinley and you say you've got to put it in per-perspective . . . "

"Perspective." Hannah smiled. "Well, not quite like that, darling."

I left Hannah to explain the difference and moved to the other side of the carriage. We were passing close to a steep embankment, moving in and out of dazzling sunlight; great tumbled rocks, upholstered in mosses and lichens, passed within inches of the window. I looked for examples of wildlife not found on the coast.

Minutes later I saw movement in the umbrageous undergrowth: a fleet, darting shape that seemed to be keeping pace with the trajectory of the cable car. As soon as I noticed one figure, I suddenly registered more, a dozen of the slim-limbed, blond humanoids, the natives of the planet: the Ashentay.

They flowed through the forest, moving with fluid motion over rocks and fallen tree trunks, their dexterity made all the more amazing by the fact that they never took their eyes off the carriage. In fact, they seemed to be staring directly at me.

Hannah was at my side. "Odd," she said. "They don't remind me in the least of Kee. They seem . . . I don't know . . . like wild animals."

I recalled the encounter with the tribe of mountain Ashentay eight years ago, how physically human they appeared, but how utterly alien they were beneath the superficial veneer of physiology.

"Some of the tribes of the interior have no contact with humans," I said. "Some tribes even refuse to have anything to *do* with the tribes that have contact with us."

"Strange," she said. Then, "Did I ever tell you, David—there's no record of a native ever having committed a crime."

I laughed. "A detective's dream."

"I don't know. If humanity were like the Ashentay, I'd be out of a job."

"Look!" Ella called from across the carriage.

We joined her. The cable car was slowing as it approached the station overlooking the great spume of the waterfall. Low timber buildings occupied a shelf of land at the terminus; viewing decks projected out over the Falls, occupied by a dozen or so awed tourists.

A tall, dark woman in the trim green uniform of Meredith Holidays met us on the platform. "Hannah van Harben and David Conway? I'm Suzanna Da Souza. I'll show you to your villa and settle you in." She knelt and touched Ella's chin. "And you must be Ella. Welcome to Tamara Falls."

Ella smiled shyly at the woman, who stood and led the way to a series of timber stairs that switch-backed up the incline. When we were almost at the head of the Falls, parallel with the curved mass of water as it tipped from the river above, Da Souza indicated ahead through the foliage. "And this is your villa . . . "

It was said more as a pronouncement, a fanfare, and I could see why.

A forecourt extended on a cantilever out over the falls, which was impressive enough, but more so was the dwelling itself. Imagine a free-form mass of molten glass allowed to find its own way between tree-trucks and over rocks; imagine that the glass was hollowed out and fitted with expensive furnishings, soft lighting and tasteful works of art.

Hannah gasped. "I . . . I don't know what to say. It's beautiful. The brochure didn't capture half its . . . " She shook her head, lost for words.

Ella, with the down-to-earth practicality of a five-year-old, piped up, "But does it have a swimming pool?"

Da Souza smiled. "You'll find the pool on the roof, in the shade of some shola trees."

She turned to us. "The complex comprises five bedrooms and three extensive communal areas, bars, kitchens, fully stocked with provisions—in fact everything you'll need for a complete break. There are also restaurants and bars down at the station. I'll be your guide to the area for the next week so I'll be in contact when your friends arrive a little later to arrange your guided tour of the archaeological dig. I'll be delighted to show you around when you've fully settled in."

She said farewell and left us to choose our rooms. We wandered through the complex like tourists in wonderland. The interior was just as impressive as the exterior, with flowing floors and walls, elevated and sunken rooms, every one of which was designed to give an optimum view of the rainforest and waterfall.

When we'd unpacked, Ella insisted on exploring. We took a short walk along timbered cat-walks and over swaying rope bridges, and I gripped Ella's hand with typical parental over-anxiety.

At one point we emerged on a mossy knoll high above the Falls. Ella darted ahead and knelt, peering into what looked like an over-sized rabbit hole. She made to scramble inside before I restrained her.

"Aw!"

"You don't know what's down there," I said.

"Let's go back and have a snack," Hannah suggested, and my daughter's butterfly mind alighted on that delight, the rabbit hole forgotten.

As I was turning from the hole, I saw sudden movement in the foliage beyond: I turned in time to see a small, blonde figure retreat further into the undergrowth and vanish. I shivered, still spooked, I told myself, from the apparition last night.

I rejoined Hannah and Ella and looked forward to meeting up with my friends later that day.

———

We were relaxing by the pool, in the shade of the shola trees, Ella splashing about with glee, when I heard voices drifting up from below.

From our vantage point we could see over the voluptuous curves of the dwelling to the cantilevered timber patio: Da Souza was giving Matt and Maddie, Hawk and Kee the company spiel. I waited until she'd left, then made my way through the house and down the steps that led from the entrance.

I hadn't seen my friends for more than six months, which was way too long, and I had anticipated this reunion for weeks. I felt the pressure of delight in my chest as I crossed the patio and hugged Maddie to me, surprised yet again at the slight, bird-boned delicacy of the tiny Englishwoman with the feisty temperament; then I shook Matt's hand and pulled him to me in a long embrace.

"You don't know how good it is to see you, Matt! I've missed you all."

"It's great to be home, David."

Hawk was next, and I had to reach up ridiculously to fully embrace the piratical giant: he was solid and iron-muscled, his flesh augmented by rigid spars and ports with which he accessed the flight-deck of his ship: the must of sweat and engine oil seemed to perpetually cling to him.

Kee dithered in the background, congenitally shy.

"Come here, you!" I said, and pulled her to me. She is even slighter than Maddie, like a twelve-year-old human girl, and I can never look at her without being reminded of my daughter Carrie, thirteen when she died.

Hannah and Ella joined us, and I watched with pride and happiness, a lump of some pleasant emotion in my throat, as a new round of greetings began.

"My," Maddie said, "how you've grown, Ella!" She looked up at Hannah. "It's amazing—just six months and she's shot up."

"And got a lot cheekier, too," I said.

Maddie grinned at Ella. "Do you know, I brought something back for you from Sirius II. If you're a good girl, I'll give it to you after dinner."

Ella beamed and gripped Maddie's hand.

I gestured at the "retort" dwelling. "Well, what do you think?"

Matt scanned it with an aesthetic eye. "My God, it's beautiful, isn't it? And the setting . . . I need this break, David."

Hawk said, "How about we freshen up then go down to one of the restaurants for a meal and a drink?"

"I don't think anyone'll oppose that suggestion," I said. "Carried?"

An hour later we were sitting around a big table on a verandah overlooking the rainbow-spangled waterfall. The conversation flowed, along with the beer. I can't even recall what we ate—all I do remember is how wonderful it was to be back in the company of the people who, beside Hannah and Ella, mattered most to me. I sat back, pleasantly drunk, and listened to Maddie's stories of their tour around the Expansion, the wondrous planets she and Matt had visited.

Then it was Hawk's turn to describe his travels, his humorous stories of the obnoxious rich tourists whose whims he'd had to accommodate. They asked about life in Magenta Bay, and I found myself recounting the small events, the incidents and dramas, of our beloved backwater township, and I realised something as I was speaking. For all my four friends had travelled the Expansion, seen sights and experienced things I never would see or experience, I could see that they'd missed life in the Bay and wished they'd been a part of the day-to-day happenings I reported with a little exaggeration.

At one point I raised my glass. "I'd just like to say a big thank you to Matt. This was a marvellous idea for a reunion. To Matt."

We drank.

Matt said, "Well, when Dr Petronious—the man with more money than many a colony world—made the offer for the show . . . " He shrugged. "How could I say no? He's a well-known patron of the arts, with his own galleries and exhibition centres across the Expansion. I know my work will be well presented."

I've known Matt for the better part of fifteen years, and I thought I detected, in his words about his benefactor, a slight hint—the merest suggestion—of resentment. I filed the observation away and decided to question Matt about it when an opportune moment arose.

I held Ella to me as she dozed and stroked Hannah's leg with my free hand. She was laughing at something Maddie had said, and telling her about a particularly funny incident that had occurred in Mackinley a while ago.

We were finishing the meal with brandy and whisky—imported from Earth—when my com chimed: Da Souza. I placed the device in the middle of the table and our guide smiled out at us.

"I hope you don't mind my interrupting. I said I'd call in and go through the tour options with you."

"The dig," Maddie said, bright-eyed.

Hawk said as an aside to Matt, "How the hell did you swing it, Matt? I thought the underground site was off-limits to plebs like us."

Matt grunted. "Thank Dr Petronious."

Da Souza was saying, "We could take a trip to the dig tomorrow afternoon, if you wish. The next time-slot after that—I have to work around the archaeologists—would be in three days."

"There's no time like the present," Hannah said.

Maddie backed her up. "I've been dying to see the dig for weeks. Let's do it tomorrow."

We agreed and Da Souza said, "That's settled, then. I'll pick you up at one tomorrow afternoon." She cut the connection.

Soon after that, with the Ring of Tharssos lighting our way, we left the restaurant and retraced our steps up wooden walkways and across rope bridges to our spectacular hilltop villa.

We slipped Ella into bed and then Hannah and I sat on the balcony outside our room, just taking in the ambience. The Ring of Tharssos bathed the scene in silver, and the almost fluorescent spume of the waterfall contrasted with the surrounding darkness of the vegetation. Another unique feature of the villa was the encapsulating sound baffle, reducing the thunderous roar of the water to nothing more than a background murmur.

After a while Hannah yawned and said she was turning in. I said I'd join her shortly, and sat admiring the view and listening to the night sounds from the rainforest: the almost mechanical ticking of an army of invisible insects, the throaty rumble of things that sounded like toads.

I saw movement on the patio below, and half expected to see the slim form of an Ashentay. The figure was slim, but it was not a native. Maddie crossed the timber boards, holding a drink, and paused before the balcony.

She smiled up at me. "Can't sleep?"

"Just admiring the view," I said.

"Mind if I have a word?"

"No, of course not." I joined her on the patio and we sat at a table near the rail. She offered to get me a drink, but I was inebriated enough after the whisky.

"I'm fine, Maddie," I said. "Is something wrong?"

She worried her bottom lip with small, perfect teeth before smiling at me and saying, "It's Matt. He's . . . " She stopped.

I recalled his manner over dinner, when talking about his patron.

"Is this something to do with Dr Petronious?" I asked.

Maddie smiled at me. "Do you know, David Conway, for someone who likes to present a bluff, rough, uneducated exterior to the world, you don't miss anything, do you?"

"I've known Matt for so long . . . " I shrugged. "He seemed bothered about something . . . his relationship with this Petronious character?"

"He was fine for most of the trip. He never likes travelling with his exhibitions—the whole media thing leaves him cold. But he was coping, and we had plenty of time to do the things we wanted, see the sights, visit people. I'd say Matt was on good form," Maddie said.

"Then he met Dr Petronious?"

"We were on Bokotar, Sirius II. It's an odd place, mostly desert, much of it too hot for habitation. The colonists there are a strange people, insular, suspicious. They've adapted to their inimical world and think themselves superior because of it."

"And Petronious is from Bokotar?"

Maddie shook her head. "No, Dr Petronious isn't human. He's from Antares II."

"Aren't they—"

She nodded. "They're a reptilian race, humanoid in form, though."

"What did you make of him?"

"Oh, I found Petronious utterly charming. Urbane, witty, sophisticated, and he possessed a phenomenal knowledge of human art. For an alien, he struck me as very . . . humane."

"What happened?"

"We met Petronious at the opening of Matt's exhibition on Bokotar; Matt had heard of him—he's one of the most influential patrons on the art scene—but had never met him. A few days later he contacted Matt and arranged a meeting. I wasn't there, but Matt told me later about Petronious's offer. He wanted to buy the ten-year exhibition rights to Matt's pieces for over three million standard credits."

I whistled. "And Matt agreed, but then had second thoughts, right? He thought he was selling out?"

Maddie pursed her lips, considering. "I . . . no, I wouldn't say that. He seemed happy with the deal. Petronious has good taste and access to all the best art venues. Matt was sure his work would get maximum coverage around the Expansion . . . But he seemed, I don't know . . . withdrawn after Bokotar, as if he was worried about something. I asked him about it—" she laughed "—I thought he'd finally got sick of me! He was upset by that, asked me how I could think such a thing. But he claimed he was fine, not worried about a thing. So," she lifted her hands in a helpless gesture, "I don't know if I'm worrying over nothing, being paranoid . . . "

I reached out and took her small hand. "I'll talk to Matt, see if I can work out what's bothering him. If anything is, of course. In the meantime, let's enjoy the break, okay?"

Maddie smiled and raised her glass. "To the break," she said, "and to friends."

We chatted for a little longer, then Maddie yawned tipsily, kissed me and said goodnight. I returned to the bedroom and rolled into bed beside Hannah; she turned to me and, half asleep, hugged me close.

Sleep was a long time coming that night. I lay awake, thinking through my encounter with the Yall apparition back at the *Mantis* . . . When I was finally dropping off I thought I glimpsed, through the diaphanous walls of the room, a pair of wide, green Ashentay eyes staring in at me.

FOUR

THE FOLLOWING MORNING we breakfasted on the balcony of our room, watching silver birds dart into the wall of the waterfall and emerge with flip-flapping golden fish. Later we sat beside the pool on the roof of the complex, in the shade of the trees, and watched Ella swim in the shallows. I had insisted that she learn to swim at the age of two, after what had happened to Carrie all those years ago, and to my delight she had taken to water like the proverbial fish.

Hawk and Kee joined us. Hawk carried a tray bearing a jug and glasses, and we sat around the pool, chatting and drinking iced fruit juice.

Hawk drained his glass and stripped down to his swimming trucks, then dived cleanly into the water. He played with Ella, laughing and splashing in the dappled sunlight.

It was the first time I'd seen the extent of Hawk's augmentations, the implants that enabled him to interface with his ship. Silver spars and webwork sat flush with his tanned flesh, outlining his broad shoulders and the line of his spine: filaments rose from his neck and cradled the base of his skull, and ports there gave access to the implants in his cerebellum.

Compared to Hawk, his partner Kee was diminutive, elf-like. She lay beside us on the lounger, tiny in her one-piece bathing costume. I suppose, given the difference of our respective planets, evolution and cultures, it was amazing that the Ashentay should resemble humans in any way, but resemble us they did: bipedal humanoids with symmetrical facial features, the requisite number of fingers and thumbs. But they were also subtly alien, and I couldn't help staring at Kee as she lay beside us, smiling at Hawk's antics in the pool.

Her slightness bordered on anorexic-looking, and, with her almost-white hair swept back, the bulge of her eyes was emphasized. She could in no way be called pretty, but rather . . . *striking*.

Now she transferred her attention from her lover and regarded the surrounding rainforest. Her big eyes darted, and I tried to catch what she was looking at. She smiled to herself a little later, and her rather serious face was transformed.

Hannah had been watching her, evidently. "What is it, Kee?"

Without turning her gaze from the rainforest, Kee said, "They are watching us, my people."

"I've noticed them," I said. "When we were travelling up here in the cable car, and again last night."

"They are curious," Kee said. "They have little contact with humans."

Hannah said, "I've heard they don't even have much to do with the Ashentay who do mix with us humans."

Kee was a while replying. "They are a strange people," she said at last. "Almost a different race. They believe that they are the True People."

I looked at her. "The True People?"

She smiled again, her lips a little longer than any humans—and the expression on her face, then, with her exothalmic eyes and attenuated lips, was almost reptilian. "They claim that because we—my people—left the interior and moved to the coast, and took up a different way, that we no longer follow the true path, laid down by our ancestors, the True People."

Hannah propped herself up on an elbow, lifted her sunglasses and said, "What is the true path, Kee?"

"We have two differing belief systems, Hannah. My people, the coastal people, we believe that we were created by a god who selected this planet as ours. But the interior tribes, they believe that we are descended from a mighty race that once spanned the galaxy, a race with technology even more advanced than your own—but a peaceful race which used their knowledge and power to help other, less developed races."

"But how did they come to live on Ashentay?" Hannah asked.

"According to the True People's beliefs, our great forbears evolved, decided that the technological way was not the right way, and came to Chalcedony—or Ashent—as we call it, turned their back on technology and lived in union with the rainforest."

"But you don't believe that?" I said.

Kee lifted a hand. "Perhaps it is true," she said cryptically.

She lay back and closed her massive eyes, and I smiled at Hannah and watched Hawk as he emerged dripping from the pool, Ella dancing in his wake.

He flopped down beside us. "She's exhausted me. I thought we came here for a rest?"

I nearly said something along the lines that rest was a rarity when you had a child—but stopped myself. Hawk and Kee could not have children. I suspected, by the way Hawk took every opportunity to play with Ella, that he would relish being a father.

We lay in silence for a while, luxuriating under the warm spring sun and listening to the insect sounds in the rainforest. Hawk's bass rumble broke the silence a little later.

"The odd thing is, you know, I knew we were coming here."

I turned my head. "What do you mean?"

He lodged his muscled arms beneath his occipital console and stared up through the swaying rainforest canopy. "Way before Maddie contacted me and told me about Matt's suggestion, I knew."

"I never had you down as psychic, Hawk," Hannah said.

He grunted. "It was odd—not at the time, but later, when I heard from Maddie and Matt."

"Are you going to tell us," I said, "or does Hannah have to apply her interrogation techniques on you?"

Hawk laughed, sat up and took a long swig of iced juice. "We'd just landed on El Habib, Janata IV. This was about three months ago, halfway through the tour. I was ready for home then, I can tell you. Oh, the Stardrift was spectacular, but I'd rather not have done it with a bunch of pernickety tourists." He grunted again. "I'm really not good at playing the polite starship captain to a bunch of over-privileged millionaires."

"You were telling us about your remarkable prescience," Hannah reminded him.

"I'm getting there," he said. "Anyway, one night on El Habib, I had a dream. This figure approached me, said that on our return to Chalcedony we'd spend some time here, Tamara Falls. It said that my presence was vital here." He laughed. "I know, crazy! Anyway, I forgot about the dream pretty quickly—and then a couple of months later Maddie calls and suggests an all-expenses-paid holiday at Tamara Falls. Of course it brought back the dream in a rush." He gestured. "Don't ask me to explain it."

"Some coincidence," Hannah said.

"There's more. When we got back to Chalcedony, I looked into how to get here from Mackinley—I didn't fancy a five-hour monotrain ride. I found out they had a landing pad here . . . and only then did I recall something else the vision in the dream told me: that I should make the trip to the Falls in my starship."

"Did it say why?" Hannah asked.

"No, not that I recall. Anyway, that's what I did."

I let a silence develop, mulling over what he'd said, before asking, "Can you recall what this figure in your dream looked like, Hawk?"

His aquiline pirate's face mimed concentration. "Well, it wasn't human. I seem to recall it was greenish, reptilian, and extraordinarily thin . . . " He shrugged. "Like no alien I've ever seen."

I lay back and stared into the swaying foliage overhead, my heart loud in my ears. He had described, pretty accurately, the same apparition that had spoken to me that night aboard the *Mantis* . . .

The Yall.

"So here you all are," a voice called out. Maddie climbed the steps from the patio and squatted beside us. "Look at you all. What a collection of lazybones. I was up at the crack of dawn, exploring.

"And what did you find, virtuous one?" I said.

"I walked for miles along the jungle walkway."

"Miles? After all you drank last night?"

She stuck her tongue out at me. "You know I never suffer, David. Anyway, I found a few old shrines, pre-dating the first stone-working Ashentay, apparently." She waved the paper map she was holding.

"Pre-dating?" I said. "I thought there was no one here before the Ashentay."

Hawk laughed. "Where have you been, David? You don't recall all the fuss in the news a few years ago: the discovery of ancient monuments in the vicinity of Tamara Falls? It's what led to the excavations and discovery of the caverns."

I shrugged. "Must have been on Earth at the time," I said, to excuse my aberrant memory.

"We'll find out more about that this afternoon," Maddie said. "Ella, I have something for you."

"Where's Matt?" Hawk asked.

"Still snoring," Maddie said, *ooph*ing as Ella landed in her lap.

She extricated a small box from beneath my daughter and held it up on the palm of her hand. "For you, Ella, all the way from Sirius II."

"What do you say, Ella?" Hannah prompted.

"Thank you," Ella said, taking the box and hastily tearing off the wrapping paper. She set the small silver box on the edge of my lounger, knelt and opened the lid.

A small golden cone, the length of Ella's hand, sat in a plush velvet nest. "It's . . . beautiful," Ella gasped, lifting it carefully from the box. "What is it?"

Maddie laughed. "An ancient alien artefact," she said. "Now a necklace."

The cone was on a chain, and Ella looped it around her neck. The golden cone sat against her bathing suit, coruscating in the sunlight.

I pulled Ella to me and examined the necklace. The cone was engraved with a spiral, like a helter-skelter, the thread inscribed with what might have been alien hieroglyphs.

Hannah said, "It is beautiful, Maddie. Thank you."

"Don't thank me," she said. "Thank an alien art patron called Dr Petronious." She explained to Hannah who Petronious was.

"Petronious gave it to you?" I said.

Maddie nodded. "The odd thing was, he knew all about us. He'd read the book, seen the movie—he said he was very interested in our story. He'd even kept up with how we were doing: he knew you had a daughter, David, and insisted that I give this to Ella."

"That's incredibly kind of him," Hannah said.

Maddie went on, "He said it was ancient, an artefact from a race of beings now extinct."

"Christ," I said, "it must be priceless."

Maddie frowned. "I doubt it, but it was a nice gesture, whatever its value."

Ella danced around the pool, holding up the cone so that it glittered in the sunlight.

"Anyway," Maddie concluded, "I came here to see if any of you had worked up an appetite for lunch before we hie ourselves off to the dig?"

"Food!" Hawk said, unfolding his bulk from the lounger. "Lead the way."

I watched my daughter as we left the pool, and it struck me that she was mesmerised by the ancient alien artefact.

FIVE

Maria Da Souza led us away from our villa and down a series of switchback stairways that descended alongside the surging torrent of the waterfall. The aural baffles were less effective here, and the roar of the fall was like a jet engine. I brought up the rear, clutching Ella's hand and squeezing it from time to time. Her excitement at the expedition communicated itself to me through her tight grip and impatient, skipping steps.

The stairway turned left, leaving the solidity of the rock and U-turning to double back on itself, even closer now to the waterfall. The walkway was horizontal here and covered in a protective crystalline tube running with water. We were walking towards the rock face over which the Falls tipped, through the mass of water itself. The pounding roar was so loud it seemed to transcend any definition of sound to become something more physical. I was relieved when we passed under the torrent and came to the area between the rippling sheet of water and the rock itself.

Da Souza turned to us and shouted, "The entrance to the subterranean system of caves is on the other side of the Falls. There is a longer way round, but this way is more spectacular."

We turned right and walked along the rock face for perhaps two hundred metres. When we reached the far side of the Falls, Da Souza paused before a ragged rent in the rock. Set into the aperture was a solid steel door, which she unlocked. She stood aside while the others, led by Hawk, squeezed through. Hannah went before me, and I brought up the rear with Ella.

As we were passing Da Souza, she lay a hand on Ella's shoulder and said, "That's a pretty necklace. May I?"

Ella nodded, and Da Souza knelt and lifted the cone. She examined it minutely, turning it in her hand. She wore an odd expression, as if she'd seen the cone before but could not recall where.

She looked up at me. "Do you mind if I ask you where you got this, Mr Conway?"

I shrugged. "It was a gift," I said, and added as if that were not sufficient, "from an alien art dealer. Why?"

She shook her head, stood quickly, and gestured for me to descend the timber staircase that followed the precipitous natural funnel through the rock. As we walked, movement-sensitive lighting came on ahead, revealing hewn rock marked with the striations of chisels and larger cutting equipment. Behind us the roar of the waterfall diminished until it could no longer be heard. As we descended, clean, cool air enveloped us, refreshing after the rainforest humidity.

I asked Da Souza, "These cutting marks, are they alien, or—"

She shook her head. "Human. Made by the initial investigation team. I'll explain when we reach the bottom."

We descended for perhaps ten minutes and the temperature plummeted: I was glad I'd taken Da Souza's recommendation to wear a jacket.

We came to the end of the timber stairway and stood on the edge of a swelling cavern. Spotlights illuminated stalactites and stalagmites, hundreds of them stretching away into the shadows. The walls nearby were wan and flesh-coloured, and reminded me of tripe, striped here and there with rust-coloured ulcerations. It was as if we were in the gut of some gargantuan bovine creature.

Da Souza took her tour-guide stance before us.

"The caverns were discovered five years ago after a botanist uncovered the standing stones and statues in the rainforest above us. A team from the University of Mackinley searched the area for more statuary, and found the entrance through which we've just passed. It was a narrow defile then, and it's since been widened. We think the race responsible for the lower chambers had another, as yet undiscovered, entrance.

"As I was telling Maddie earlier, at first scientists thought the standing stones were of Ashentay provenance, but subsequent investigations discounted this theory."

"But there were no native peoples on the planet *before* the Ashentay," Hawk said.

Da Souza smiled. "Quite. That led researchers to speculate that the stones were of extraterrestrial origin. What archaeologists discovered down here bore out that idea. If you would care to follow me."

She set off and, intrigued, we followed.

We walked for a hundred metres and came to the end of the cavern. The walls closed in, the stalactite-spiked roof descended, and ahead I made out a dark opening, through which our guide now ducked.

Ella could walk upright through the narrow corridor, but the rest of us were forced to bend double. A sharp, dry, salty smell filled the air.

After fifty metres the corridor gave way to another chamber, this one quite different from the last.

We stood up, stretched, and let out exclamations of surprise.

In complete contrast to the natural contours of the first chamber, this one was so obviously manufactured that it was as if we'd been teleported from one locale to another. But what was even more staggering about what opened up before us was the nature of the work done down here. For some reason I had been expecting statues and carvings hewn from the rock, perhaps crude figures, effigies . . . I should have known better, of course: if a star-faring race had left vestiges of their civilisation here, then it was not likely to resemble something out of Terran antiquity.

For a start, the cavern was triangular: two great sloping walls rose to meet at a sharp point a hundred metres overhead, and the walls were fashioned not from rock but from metal, smooth and seamless. If the very shape of the cavern confounded my expectations, then so did its contents.

Hundreds of thousands of silver columns, each perhaps three centimetres in diameter and as high as a man, rose from the flat metal decking. They stood a metre from each other, like some enigmatic extraterrestrial work of art.

"But what are they?" Hawk asked.

Da Souza smiled. "The 64-million-dollar question, Mr Hawksworth. If the scientists could work that one out . . . "

I gestured towards the closest of the columns. "Can we . . . ?" I asked.

"Be my guest."

We stepped forward and touched the spears. I pulled my hand away quickly. "They're . . . *warm* . . . "

"Thirty degrees Celsius, Mr Conway. All of them."

I laid my hand on the column again, feeling its comforting heat.

Ella, with the audacity of childhood, embraced a column. "I know what they are!" she piped up. "They're alien heaters. It's cold down here!"

Da Souza laughed. "They might well be, Ella. I'll tell the scientists about your theory."

"I suppose you don't know how they're powered?" Matt asked.

"Again, we don't know. As with all alien technology, we have to be very, very circumspect . . . not only in our interpretation of what objects might be, but on a more practical level, in terms of our physical address of the objects. We don't know what we're dealing with here. For all we know, it might be as potentially dangerous as a nuclear power station."

Matt stood before the array of columns, arms folded across his chest, frowning.

I mooted my alien-work-of-art theory.

He grunted. "Too . . . too ordered, David. Too schematic." Then he laughed. "But by saying that I fall into a trap. How can I begin to interpret an alien aesthetic? It might be an art installation, for all I know, but I have a hunch it's something more . . . more mechanical."

Maddie came up to him and slipped an arm around his ample waist. "Just think, Matt, in thousands of years, aliens might be trying to interpret *your* art."

He pulled an expressive face. "Now that's an utterly depressing thought, on many levels."

"Speaking of timescales . . . " Hawk said, then addressed Da Souza, "Do the archaeologists know how old all this is? You say it predates the Ashentay."

Da Souza nodded. "Estimates range from eight hundred thousand years to a million, give or take a few thousand."

Maddie whistled.

"But whoever made this, you say they weren't native to the planet?"

"That's right, Mr Conway. No evidence of a technological civilisation has been found anywhere else on Chalcedony, not the slightest trace. That would lead one to surmise an extraterrestrial source for all this."

"But you've no hard evidence of that?" Hawk asked.

Da Souza smiled. "If you'd care to accompany me through to the next chamber . . . "

Dutifully, we followed. I caught Hannah's eye and smiled. This was far better a guided tour than I'd dare hope for.

We passed through a triangular portal, which mirrored the architecture of the chamber we were leaving, and entered an even vaster chamber.

Maddie whistled again. "This is . . . amazing."

"Daddy!" Ella cried. "What are they? They look like . . . like spaceships."

Da Souza winked at me. "You have a budding scientist there, Mr Conway. That's what we're pretty sure they are, Ella."

Hawk laughed. "An underground car park for starships!"

The vessels—if indeed they were vessels—were racked one above the other, three high: sleek silver wedges about the size of the *Mantis*. They bore no exterior markings, no seams to indicate exits or viewscreens. Even their sterns, where you might expect to see evidence of some form of propulsion, rockets or at least exhaust flarings, were without any sign of these.

I estimated there were about a hundred craft stacked in the chamber.

"Hard to credit that they might be a million years old," Maddie said.

"The dictates of aerodynamics were the same back then," Hawk replied.

"But they can't be spaceships," Ella frowned, "because they don't have doors."

I squeezed her hand. "Perhaps the aliens were very small," I said, "and they squeezed in through tiny holes?"

"Let's go and look!" she cried.

For the next ten minutes we moved around the stacked ships, examining them closely for evidence of miniature apertures.

Scattered about the ships were more prosaic items: the tables and com-terminals of the archaeologists, lending a welcome, familiar air to this wholly alien environment.

I noticed another triangular portal at the far end of the chamber, this one sealed by a makeshift plastic hatch, marked with a red and black hazard symbol.

I pointed. "What's through there?"

"Ah . . . that's strictly off limits, Mr Conway," Da Souza said.

Before I could enquire further, she looked at her watch and said, "Now, the next shift of scientists is due down here in less than an hour, so perhaps we'd better be making tracks. I trust the tour, if brief, was edifying."

We murmured our appreciation as we filed back through the chambers towards the exit stairway.

Later, as we emerged from the subterranean cool into the cloying humidity of the rainforest, Kee—who had been quiet until that point—shivered and said, "I didn't like it down there, Hawk. It was creepy."

We hurried back to the villa.

SIX

WE DECIDED TO EAT IN THAT EVENING and I made my speciality, green Thai curry. Checking the provisions in the cooler and extensive storeroom before I began, I was amazed to find all the requisite ingredients to hand; it was as if whoever had provisioned the villa had known of my culinary predilections.

They had even stocked the cooler full of our favourite beer.

We ate on the patio as they sun went down and the Ring of Tharssos brightened. As we ate and chatted, I wondered if I was not alone in sensing—despite being among my best friends at long last—an air of unease hovering over us like a storm cloud. First there was the visitation of the Yall apparition, then Hawk's dream urging him to travel to the Falls in his starship, Petronious's gift of the cone necklace and Da Souza's odd reaction to seeing it—not to mention Kee's shivery assessment of what we had seen underground. I think she had spoken for all of us then.

If we were aware of the finger of fate directing us towards who knew what outcome, we did our best not to acknowledge it. Conversation was light, jocular; Hawk told disparaging stories about the tourists he'd shepherded around the Expansion and Hannah chipped in with some of the more light-hearted stories of life in the Mackinley police department. Even Kee joined in with a story recounting Hawk's embarrassment when he snubbed a minor royal at a party on the newly-settled colony world of Runciman, Aldebaran VI.

Spluttering on his beer, Hawk laughed, "How the hell was I supposed to know? I thought he was a waiter!"

"It's true," Kee giggled. "Hawk asked him to refill my glass!"

The night proceeded in this fashion as the stars came out, a blazing panoply of brilliance high above the Ring. It was a good night, just like old times, but I couldn't help but notice that one of our number was uncharacteristically quiet: Matt smiled and on occasion even laughed, but he didn't join in with stories of his own, or offer dry comments. It was not like him. He seemed to hold himself apart from the conversation, observing.

At one point I asked my friends about what we'd seen in the subterranean chamber. "Did you get the impression that Da Souza wasn't telling us everything down there?"

"I'm sure she wasn't," Hawk said. "I'm sure the boffins have discovered a hell of a lot more than she told us."

"Isn't that to be expected, after all?" Maddie asked.

"Of course," I said, "it's just that . . . "

Hannah was looking at me with professional eyes. She leaned forward and said, "You had words with Da Souza on the way down, David. And after that her manner was . . . let's say cagey. What did you say to her? Out with it."

I wondered if I could ever hide anything from my wife.

"Well, it wasn't so much what I said . . . " And I went on to tell them about Da Souza's reaction to seeing Ella's alien necklace. "It was almost as if she'd seen it before," I finished.

Out of the corner of my eye, I saw Matt lean forward minimally and open his mouth as if to say something. He thought better of it and leaned back. I glanced at him, but he looked away and drained the last of his beer.

I knew better than to quiz him then. Maybe later, I thought, when we were alone.

Maddie said, "Perhaps she *has* seen something like it before: what of it?"

I shrugged. "I don't know. Perhaps I was wrong. It just struck me as odd—I mean, if she did recognise the necklace, surely she would have commented?"

"You're drunk, David Conway. You're reading more into a casual remark than was really there," Hannah said.

I shrugged. Beside me, Ella said tiredly, "Daddy's not drunk, are you! The lady did look at my necklace. I think she knew it was worth millions and millions of creds!" She lifted the cone and stared at it, and a little later slipped from the table and went to play in the garden next to the patio.

I turned to Kee, "Do you know if the Ashentay knew anything about the underground chamber?"

Her reaction surprised me; she looked away pointedly and said, "I'm sure they didn't know anything about it, David."

Conversation moved on and the beer flowed; it was just before midnight when the first yawn set us all off; the gathering broke up and we made for our respective rooms. I told Hannah I'd put Ella to bed, and moved to the adjacent flower garden.

Ella was sitting cross-legged on the lawn before a border, poking at something with a stick. I dropped down beside her.

"And what's happening here?"

"Daddy, they're not doing what I want them to do."

I smiled. "What aren't, bean?"

"These . . . these creatures!"

I leaned forward and stared at where she was pointing with the stick. In the silvery ring-light I made out scurrying red ant-like insects, half the size of my thumb.

"Look, there's a juicy bit of sava fruit here and I want them to find it and take it into their house . . ." She indicated the opening to their underground lair. "But they just ignore it. Look, they're going round it. Even when I put the fruit right in front of them. Aren't they hungry?"

I smiled. "It's not they aren't hungry, Ella. Just that these particular . . . chivills, they're called . . . are nest builders. They have a duty, and it's to gather material to build their house. Now these chivills over here . . ." I pointed to a foraging party. "I think these might be interested in the fruit."

"You think so?"

"Why not find out? Put the fruit there . . ."

With the stick she prodded the windfall across the soil and into the path of the foraging chivills. A dozen of them swarmed over it, got a grip and managed to roll it towards the entrance to their lair. Seconds later it was gone.

Ella clapped her hands in delight.

I pulled her into my lap, kissed her soft cheek and said, "Right. It's way past your bedtime."

"Story?"

"A short one, if you hurry up to bed this minute."

I put Ella to bed, made up a quick story about chivills in search of giant sava fruit, then joined Hannah on the balcony of our room.

I reached out and held her hand. We sat in silence for a while, as if awed by the natural beauty around us. Hannah said, very quietly, "What's happening, David?"

I knew better than to fob her off. I said, "I honestly don't know."

She was silent for a while. "David," she said at last, "what is it about you, your group of friends?"

I looked at her.

"They're special," she said, "aren't they?"

I squeezed her hand. "Not as special—" I began.

"You know what I mean. They're . . . I mean, look what happened six years ago, with Matt and that Dortmund character. And before that—you told me about the Ashentay bone-smoking ritual and what happened then. And before that, the Opening of the Way. What is it about you people?"

I shrugged, at a loss to explain the incidents that had swept us up and carried us along, often against our will.

She said, almost in a whisper, "And it's happening again, isn't it?"

I was blithe. "Oh, I don't know about that."

"Treat me with a little respect, David!" she snapped. "Look, I know something's going on. Ever since the night before we came here. The night you couldn't sleep: you were talking to . . . something in the kitchen . . . " She turned her deep green eyes on me. "Are you going to tell me, David?"

So I sighed and told her about the apparition, and what the Yall had said to me.

When I finished, Hannah shivered and said, "I'm frightened."

I reached out. "Don't be. I was being honest when I said I don't know what's going on. But I do know that I trust the Yall. It told me to be prepared, but not to fear. It said that all will be well."

She smiled. "I hope so, David."

We went to bed and made love slowly, with tenderness; I caressed her with touches that meant more than mere words, trying to communicate to Hannah that no matter what happened, no matter what events overtook us in the days to come, the reality of our union was the thing that mattered most to me.

While she breathed gently in sleep beside me, I lay awake. An hour passed, then two. I stared at the clock embedded in the glass wall, watching the seconds slowly elapse. At last, at almost three in the morning, I got up, pulled on my shorts and shoes, and fetched a sava juice from the bar.

I sat on the balcony in the cooling night breeze, drank slowly and marvelled at the sweep of stars overhead.

I became aware, by degrees, that the movement in the jungle was more than just the casual rustle of small animals about their nocturnal business. The sounds were quiet but regular, soft footfalls coming from every direction. Perhaps I should have felt some measure of alarm, but the odd fact was that I felt very calm, as if possessed by some strange foreknowledge that whatever happened I would come to no harm.

I stared into the rainforest, the silvered leaves contrasting with the inky shadows between them. Occasionally I caught a glimpse of a running body, fleet in the ring-light, and once or twice I fancied I saw a flash of eyes, staring out at me.

The activity increased. I sensed that the villa was surrounded by the curious native folk: I had never felt more observed in my life.

I drank my juice unperturbed.

Five minutes later I was startled by a relatively loud sound from my right. I glanced across the patio. A door had opened, and a figure emerged.

Kee padded across the timber deck and paused before the fringe of the rainforest. She seemed to be peering into the foliage, waiting . . .

I was aware that I was holding my breath in anticipation of what was about to happen.

The odd thing was, I *knew* that Kee was standing there below me not because she had heard the noises and was curious, but because she had been summoned . . . or perhaps this is no more than the wisdom of hindsight.

Suddenly, surprising me, two figures emerged from the foliage before Kee, took her arms and led her into the rainforest. She seemed to accompany them with reluctance, leaning back against their grip as she vanished into the shadows. I heard the rustling of others in the surrounding jungle, the noise receding as they followed Kee.

I was sweating. My first impulse was to alert Hawk, my second—which for some reason I obeyed—was to follow Kee.

I moved quickly from the balcony, crossed the patio and came to the fringe of rainforest into which Kee had passed. I made out a worn path through the undergrowth, no more than a run made by small animals. I stepped forward, feeling the forest loam give gently under the soles of my canvas shoes, and hurried up the path after the fleeing Ashentay, batting away swaying fronds and the occasional curious airborne insect.

I came to a wider path—the same one Maddie told us she'd followed the other day—and caught a flash of movement up ahead: the Ashentay, perhaps a dozen of them.

They were swarming up a steep incline, much swifter than I could hope to run. I gave chase, panting, but not for one second questioning either the wisdom or the logic of what I was doing.

I arrived at the crest of the incline and looked about. The pathway continued to my right, and I followed it. Fifty metres further on I came to a clearing and halted quickly.

I knelt, breathing hard from the exertion, and stared through a fan of ferns.

This was evidently the place where, yesterday, Maddie had found the standing stone.

It rose from the mossy clearing, outlined in the silver ring-light, perhaps the height of a man and twice as broad. From this distance

I could see engravings etched on its flank, but I was too far away to make them out with any accuracy.

More interesting, however, was what the gathered Ashentay were doing. I counted twelve of them, slight beings dressed only in loinclothes, plus Kee who wore her customary yellow slip.

The aliens were encircling the stone, their hands linked; Kee was among them, taking part in this ritual—if a ritual it was—as if familiar with the procedure. As I watched, a soft, feathery twittering passed around the circle, as each of them in turn uttered quiet words: when it came to Kee's turn, to my surprise she lowered her head and spoke.

Seconds later the ritual appeared to be over. They unclasped hands, the chain broken, and turned to leave the clearing.

I was taken then by the desire to get away, not wanting to be seen spying on whatever they had been doing. I turned and ran, and my retreat was far faster than the outward journey. I skidded and careered down the incline, almost falling over more than once, eager that my flight should not be seen.

It seemed only seconds later that I arrived back, bursting onto the patio like a clown onto a stage. I stopped, as much to muster dignity as to catch my breath, then hurried over to the table and sat down.

Seconds later I heard movement in the rainforest and Kee emerged, alone, through the fronds. She padded across the decking, staring ahead as if in a daze. I got to my feet and stood before her so that I impeded her progress. She stopped before me, staring at my chest. I reached out; touched her shoulder. "Kee?"

She seemed drugged, her eyes wide, unseeing.

I shook her. "Kee?" I said again.

She gave not the slightest response, and I thought it wise not to wake her. I stood aside, and she continued on her way and slipped through the door to her room. I stood for a while in the ring-light, my heart beating feverishly, before I moved from the patio.

This time, oddly, sleep claimed me within minutes.

SEVEN

THE FOLLOWING MORNING, over communal breakfast, Maddie announced that she was going to take us on a tour of the area.

She'd made a picnic and we stowed sandwiches and beer in our backpacks then set off from the villa. Instead of taking the walkway down the side of the Falls, as we had yesterday, Maddie led us up the timber construction. Within minutes we were above the great roaring crest of the waterfall. We stood on an observation platform jutting out over where the river tipped over the edge of the escarpment, and the noise was like a physical assault.

Ella squealed in delight and pointed to a host of dare-devil swordbills plunging into the water on the very edge of the waterfall and emerging, with laboured flapping of wings, from the wave-front seconds later bearing struggling fish.

"I've been doing some calculations!" Maddie shouted. "To give you some idea of how big the river is: the content of Magenta Bay tips over the edge every five seconds."

I stared at the spume-wreathed falls in wonder.

Maddie consulted a folding plastic map and pointed away from the Falls. "There's a marked path leading into the rainforest. It loops to take us back to the villa. I reckon the round trip should take a couple of hours. At mid-point," she indicated a grassy knoll rising above the trees, "we could stop for lunch."

We set off, Maddie leading the way.

I brought up the rear, Hannah in front of me with Ella. As we walked, I watched Kee next to Hawk, diminutive by comparison. She seemed quiet, subdued; but then, I told myself, that was her default state. I had never known her to be lively or loquacious.

I tried to forget the incident of the night before, and the many other odd events of late, and enjoy the walk.

Not only was Chalcedony blessed with a marvellously temperate climate at this latitude, but no predatory or poisonous animals existed to spoil the touristic wonderland. The planet had little industry—all necessary manufactured goods were telemassed in—and its main revenue was from tourism. It was a big world, thankfully, so the many millions of visitors a year were spread thinly across its six vast continents. We saw not one other visitor that day, but plenty of native wildlife.

A little over an hour after setting off, we came to the nub of land butting through the tree canopy. Hawk made it to the top ahead of everyone else, and stood with his arms braced on one knee like a triumphant mountaineer of old. "Would you look at the view!" he said as we joined him.

Maddie gasped, and Hannah laughed in uninhibited delight. She gripped my hand. "David, I've never seen anything like it. It's . . . it's beautiful!"

We could see for hundreds of kilometres in every direction. Behind us, the rainforest extended to the horizon, an uninterrupted, undulating carpet of variegated greens. To our left was the blue gash of the river, crossed with a margin of white spume, like a horizontal cloud seen from this vantage point, where it plunged over the escarpment. Ahead of us was the central mountain range.

Before it, geometrically perfect in its ramrod-straight, three-kilometre length, was the Golden Column. As we watched, the tiny shapes of starcraft approached the light and disappeared into it. I thought I could sit here for hours, watching the distant activity.

We broke out the picnic and ate.

Ella sat in the bowl of my crossed legs, chomping on a sandwich and passing me the crust with the hauteur of royalty dispensing largesse. When I dutifully hoovered it up, she prodded my belly and said to Hannah, "Mummy, Daddy's getting fat!"

"No wonder, the way you feed him scraps."

Ella was thoughtful for a while, then said, "Hawk?"

Hawk was stretched out full length, head propped on a hand. "Mmm?"

"Do you know those alien spaceships under the waterfall? Well, how did they get there? You know all about spaceships."

"That's a very good question, Ella. I was wondering the same thing myself." He sat up, popped a beer and gestured with it. "Two solutions, as far as I can make out. The guide said the chamber might have been a million years old—well, perhaps that long ago the chamber wasn't underground, but at ground level. Perhaps it was open-ended, like a hangar. That's one possibility." He looked around the group to see if we agreed; no one objected. "Now the other possibility is that the aliens, whoever they were, had a form of teleportation, either like our own, or the Yall's Golden Column. That would explain how they could secrete their ships in a sealed chamber—if it *was* underground all those millennia ago." He shrugged. "Well that's my guess, anyway."

"Or perhaps," Ella said, "the silver ships aren't spaceships at all. Maybe they're digging machines and they dug all the way down there!"

"Well," Hawk said with judicious appreciation of his half-full bottle, "there's always that possibility."

Ella grinned up at me, proud of her deductive powers.

We finished eating and lazed around for a while in the spring sunlight. Ella found another insect nest to inspect, and Maddie and Hannah chatted about something, their voices a pleasant drone on the edge of my consciousness. Matt sat off to one side, staring out towards the Golden Column, a beer cradled in his lap.

I moved across to him. "You okay, Matt?"

He glanced at me, smiled. "I'm fine, David. Tired, that's all. Dog tired. The trip took it out of me. I thought it'd be easy, physically, if not mentally."

"And it wasn't?"

He shook his head and took a swallow of beer. "Mentally it was the same as ever: the same routine, receptions, a million meetings with eager individuals I'd never meet again, a thousand interviews . . . But *physically* . . . it left me feeling shattered, to be honest, drained."

"Well," I said, "you can take a few months off, presumably?"

He laughed. "That's just what I intend to do, David—until the guilt at my lack of productivity starts gnawing again, and I get another idea, and start work. But I shouldn't complain—I have the best job and lifestyle in the Expansion."

I liked Matt Sommers more than words could express. I liked his gentleness, his quietly-spoken humanity, his humility. He was one of the most feted artists in the Expansion, a very rich man who, without telling anyone other than his close friends (and only then because Maddie let it slip in a drunken moment last year) gave hundreds of thousands to various charities on Earth and the colonies. He shunned publicity and was loyal to those he considered close.

I wondered if tiredness at the recently completed tour was the sole reason for his silence, his withdrawn state of late.

Maddie stood and, like a roistering Sergeant Major, gave the order to break camp and continue the hike.

We packed our backpacks and set off down from the summit of the grassy hilltop, passing from direct sunlight into the dappled cover of the rainforest. Strange, plangent birdsong sounded, a gulping double note that sounded both loud and yet far away.

Kee looked up, smiling at us. "The zandikine bird," she announced. "It's very rarely heard. My people say that hearing it brings good fortune."

As we walked, Ella pointed out a host of iridescent insects swimming through the humid air, catching the rays of the sun as they went. I was alert for the attention of the Ashentay, but for all my vigilance I caught neither sight nor sound of the forest-dwellers.

Thirty minutes later Maddie paused and pointed down the incline. Through a gap in the trees we could see the villa, perhaps half a kilometre away, the free-form, Dali-esque blobs of its multiple rooms seeming to inhabit the rainforest like some natural, sap-like substance.

Ahead, the path forked. Maddie consulted the map and pointed to the left fork. "This will take us to the standing stone I mentioned the other day. The right-hand path is the quicker way back to the villa."

I said, "I wouldn't mind taking a look at the stone." I looked at Kee; she gave no reaction to my preference.

The others agreed and we set off down the left-hand path.

Ten minutes later we entered the clearing where last night Kee and her fellow Ashentay had performed the enigmatic alien ritual.

We crossed to the standing stone, phallic in the intermittent light of the sun.

I paused before it, examining the carved relief on its flank. "Are they figures?" Hannah said. She pointed to what might have been a bi-pedal form, almost too faint to be seen, perhaps as tall as my little finger. Around it, swirling patterns had been etched into the rock,

I looked up at Kee, who was standing, watching us, some metres away. "What do you think this might be?" I asked her.

She turned a hand, her people's substitution for a shrug, and said, "I don't know, David."

"Did you come here with Maddie the other day?"

She shook her head. "No." She was silent for a few seconds, then, "I have never been here before . . . " But I could see, from something in her eyes, that she was doubting the veracity of the statement. I wondered if she truly could not recall the events of the previous night.

Maddie said excitedly, "David! Here!"

She was on the other side of the stone, tracing the upper half of a second figure. She looked up. "Am I seeing things, or is that . . . " She tapped a fingernail against the figure's torso.

I knelt, but the light was so bad that I could hardly make out the carving, never mind its decoration. "Hawk," I said, "could you just move that damned a tree a little to the left."

Obligingly, he mimed pushing it. "That any better?"

Maddie laughed. "Would you believe it, it is!"

A shaft of accidental sunlight pierced the canopy then and illuminated the standing stone.

I examined the figure. "There," Maddie said. "Am I seeing things, or is the figure wearing a necklace like Ella's?"

Around the figure's neck I could just make out a faint line, and hanging from it what might have been—with a little imagination—the alien cone. I wasn't convinced, however.

I glanced at Hannah, whose eyesight was better than mine. "What do you think?"

She peered. "Well, it could be . . . "

Everyone stepped up to take a look, and opinion was split. "You're imagining things, Maddie," Matt said.

Hawk disagreed, "I don't know, I think it does look like *a* cone . . . "

"It is!" Ella said. "It's my necklace, Mummy!"

I glanced at Kee. "What do you think?"

She came forward, almost reluctantly, and peered at the figure. "I think it's a shola cone," she pronounced, matter-of-factly.

Hawk laughed. "Well, that would be a more likely explanation."

Five minutes later we left the clearing and made our way back to the villa.

That night we elected to dine at a different restaurant down the hillside, this one a glass extrusion that bled over the side of the falls. We occupied a private bubble off the main bar and, disconcertingly, we could look down through the floor and view the boiling river far below.

Whether it was because of the off-putting view, the fact that I'd eaten a lot on the picnic, or the cuisine—an odd Martian–Terran fusion—I had little appetite and picked at my food. Towards the end of the meal Hawk suggested we take our beers out onto the projecting balcony. Matt seconded the notion and the three of us left Hannah, Maddie and Kee—with Ella curled fast asleep on a lounger—discussing politics in the private bubble.

The balcony was a wide ledge a metre from the surging spray, silenced by aural baffles. Other diners were taking in the view. Further along the balcony I noticed Maria Da Souza, drink in hand, chatting to a uniformed colleague.

Hawk said, apropos of nothing, "I think we need to talk."

I glanced at Matt, who nodded. "I'm not sure I know what's going on here," I began.

Hawk said, "But something is 'going on', isn't it?"

Matt looked at Hawk. "Have you told David about what you saw—or dreamed—while you were away?"

"I know about it," I said. "And . . . just a day before we came here, I was visited again by a Yall. In my ship." I recounted my encounter with the apparition, and told Matt and Hawk what the avatar had told me.

"'Be prepared,'" Matt repeated. "'Do not fear. All will be well.' Christ, what the hell's going on?"

Hawk said, "And the cone . . . Da Souza's reaction to it. And if it *was* depicted on that standing stone . . ."

I looked at him. "I thought you doubted it *was* the cone, Hawk?"

"To be honest, I'm not so sure."

Matt took a long drink of beer and looked at us. "There's something else. Another odd fact to add to all the others. I've told you both about Dr Petronious, the Antarian art patron, his staggering offer to buy my exhibition and tour it around the Expansion . . ."

Hawk said, "What about it?"

Matt looked grimly from Hawk to me. "There was a catch," he said. "Petronious said that the deal could only go ahead if I agreed to one thing—I had to come here, to Tamara Falls, and invite the rest of you for a week, this specific week."

"And he didn't say why, right?"

"Right, he didn't say why." Matt paused. "At the time I thought it an odd request, but I couldn't see why I should let it stand in the way of an amazing offer. So I agreed . . . But since coming here, and talking to Hawk . . . and learning about your encounter with the Yall, David . . . now I'm not so sure."

I said, "'Be prepared. Do not fear. All will be well' . . . I trust the Yall. We are prepared, as well as we can prepare ourselves."

"But for what?" Hawk asked.

I looked around the balcony. Further along the rail, Da Souza was saying goodbye to her colleague. They hugged and parted, and as the woman left, Da Souza looked down at her almost empty glass as if debating whether to have another.

Something occurred to me. "One second," I told my friends. "I just want to ask our guide something."

I crossed to Da Souza. She had drained her glass and was starting towards the bar when I said, "I hope you don't mind . . . "

"Oh, Mr Conway."

I indicated her drink. "If you'd like another . . . ?"

She thought about it, then said, "No, let me get this one. I insist. And your friends?" She signalled across to Hawk and Matt with a raised glass. They raised their own in acknowledgment.

Da Souza made her way to the bar and I rejoined Matt and Hawk. "What did you want to ask her? Hawk asked.

"About the necklace," I said.

Da Souza crossed the transparent floor of the balcony bearing a tray with three beers and a gin and tonic. She raised her glass and said, "I hope you're enjoying your break, gentlemen."

"It's a quite remarkable place," I said.

She beamed. I got the impression that the gin wasn't her second, or even her third. She swayed a little as she smiled, eyeing Hawk's muscular chest with ill-concealed attraction. Hawk had this effect on women, and he returned her smile and said, "David was just telling us about his daughter's necklace. The alien cone."

Da Souza blinked and looked at me. I said, "Yesterday, before we entered the cavern. You commented on it, and I thought you'd seen it before somewhere." I smiled. "Now I know. On the standing stone in the clearing, right?"

She pursed her lips, as if trying to recall which standing stone I was talking about. "The standing stone?" She shook her head. "No. No, it wasn't there."

Matt said, quickly, "But you have seen it before?"

Da Souza seemed to be considering her words. At length she said, "Yes, that's right. I have."

"Do you mind telling us where?" Hawk asked.

She pursed her lips around another mouthful of gin, and finally nodded. "A few years ago, just after the discovery was made and word got out about what had been found, we had a request from someone very influential: he wanted to visit the chamber. And he was willing to pay a substantial amount to be accorded the privilege."

Matt glanced at me. "What happened?"

"His request was turned down."

"On what grounds?" Hawk wanted to know.

"Well, the individual was an Antarian, you see."

Hawk blinked. "He was turned down because he was an alien?" he said disbelievingly.

By way of an explanation, Da Souza said, "We run the Falls in close co-operation with the Ashentay Elders on Chalcedony, Mr Hawksworth. They have a very large say in what happens here, how we run things, who we allow to visit. In fact, they have the ultimate veto."

Hawk shook his head. "And they didn't want this individual to visit because he was Antarian?"

Da Souza nodded. "That's right."

Matt said, "But did they give you a reason?"

"No reason was officially given, but I heard a rumour that a long time ago, millennia ago, there was some . . . enmity, let's say, between the races." She shrugged. "But that's only gossip, I must stress."

Matt was looking thoughtful. "And the identity of this mysterious, wealthy Antarian . . . ?" he asked. "A certain Mr Petronious, at a guess?"

Da Souza halted her glass halfway to her lips. "How do you know that, Mr Sommers?"

"We're acquainted," Matt explained.

"But . . . you said you recognised the cone necklace?" I reminded her.

"That's right. You see, Mr Petronious made a visit to Chalcedony especially to make his request. He went before the board of the Meredith Organisation. I was on hand to show him around. And he was wearing, around his neck, the necklace bearing the golden cone. And then yesterday I saw your daughter wearing something very much like it."

Matt said, "So he came here in person, with the cone. That's interesting."

Da Souza looked at me. "Where did you get the cone?" she asked.

"Oh, it was a gift," I said. "I suspect there are millions of the things in circulation around the Expansion."

Matt asked Da Souza, "What did you make of Dr Petronious?"

She frowned. "Well, I met him only for a matter of minutes. Five at the very most. And I watched his petition to the board—it was relayed to some officials in an adjacent chamber, and I was present." She hesitated.

Matt said, "Yes?"

"The odd thing was, he knew about the third chamber—the one currently off limits. It was this chamber he was especially interested in. We assumed at the time that word had leaked out—that was the only explanation."

"Do you have any idea why the third chamber should interest him so much?" I asked.

She shook her head. "He didn't say, in so many words. He just said he was a connoisseur of alien artefacts, and that he'd appreciate access to the chamber."

Matt nodded, staring into his beer, then looked up and said, "And just what is in that third chamber, Ms Da Souza?"

She knocked back her drink, then regarded Matt steadily. "As it will be opening for the first time next week anyway, just after you're due to leave . . . I don't see any harm in offering you a sneak preview."

I looked at the others, surprised. "We'd appreciate that."

"The only problem," Da Souza went on, "is that the next shift comes on at six in the morning,"

Hawk gave his most winning smile. "In that case, I don't suppose a midnight visit would be possible?" he suggested.

Da Souza returned his smile. "I can't see that any harm would come of it, Mr Hawksworth," she said. "If you meet me outside your villa in say . . . fifteen minutes?"

I nodded. "We'll be there."

Da Souza left the restaurant and we returned to the dining bubble. Maddie looked up tipsily. "Well, have you three been having fun entertaining the Amazonian Miss Da Souza?" she asked.

Kee said, seriously, "Human women find Hawk irresistibly attractive, for some reason."

"There have been developments," Matt said, cutting through the banter. "We'll fill you in on the way."

Hannah blinked. "The way? The way where?"

I said, "We're going underground again, to the alien chambers. The third chamber."

Maddie clapped her hands. "Oh, there's nothing I like more than a midnight adventure!"

Hannah said, "We can't take Ella, David. Look, she's fast asleep."

"If it is okay, Hannah, I will babysit for you. I don't want to go into the third chamber," Kee said.

Hannah nodded. I said, "If you're sure, Kee."

She stared at me. "I said, I don't want to go into the third chamber."

"Fine." I nodded. "Fine, in that case . . . "

"What are we waiting for?" Hawk said.

We returned to the villa, tucked Ella up in bed with Kee in the next room, and rendezvoused with Da Souza.

And only then, as she was leading us under the waterfall to the subterranean chambers, did I recall something she had told us earlier: that millennia ago the Ashentay and the Antarians were enemies.

But, I thought, the Ashentay had never been a star-faring race . . .

EIGHT

As we left the roar of the waterfall behind us and descended into the cool of the near-vertical stairwell, Maddie said, "Do you ever get the impression that we're being manipulated?"

I looked at her as she picked her way down the stairway before me.

"I mean," she went on, "what the Yall told you and Hawk. It's happened before, after all. We did the bidding of the Yall."

Matt said, "You know I'm no fatalist, Maddie."

She smiled at him. "You don't believe that some things are meant to be?" She gripped his hand. "Like you and me, Matt and Kee, David and Hannah? The fact that we're all friends?"

Matt laughed gruffly. "Listen to her. That's the retroactive delusion of an incurable romantic speaking."

Maddie demurred. "Romanticism isn't a disease, Matt, thank you very much."

"The odd thing is . . . " I said, thinking as I spoke, "the first time I was approached by the Yall . . . it certainly seemed as if it knew what was in store, as if it could see into the future."

"And this time, too," Maddie said. "What did the apparition say, David? About being prepared, not to fear, and that all will be well." She shook her head. "It's as if it *knows* what is about to happen."

I waved. "But how can an apparition know anything about the future?" Even as I said this, I considered the events of six years ago.

Hawk voiced my thoughts. "Remember the Ashentay bone-smoking ceremony? Look what happened then. I don't claim to understand it, but it did seem as if the ceremony allowed the participants a glimpse of future events."

I considered the painful series of events that had played themselves out in the mountains of the interior. I certainly had no explanation for what had happened then.

"I just hope," Hannah said, "that the Yall apparition was right when it said all will be well."

A silence settled after that and we followed da Souza down the stairway.

We came at last to the first chamber, and for some reason it seemed larger than I recalled: the strange forest of silver spears seemed to extend further across the floor of the cavern. An optical illusion fuelled, I considered, by tiredness and alcohol.

We passed into the second chamber, and this loomed vast and cathedral-like. I was so impressed by its dimensions this time that I came to a halt, awed, on the threshold. At the same time I was aware of another, subtler sensation: unease at the sight of the racked ships—if ships they were—and the thought that alien intelligences had constructed these chambers, millennia ago, for some purpose.

Everything—the notion of alien intent, the dimensions of the chamber—worked to make me feel very small.

I hurried after the others as they moved across the echoing cavern towards the small triangular portal at its far end, boarded by the makeshift, human hatch bearing the "Off Limits" legend.

As Da Souza scraped open the flimsy plastic door and we moved into a cavern even vaster than the last, I was not alone in feeling the temperature plunge. Beside me, Hannah shivered. Maddie said, "It's as if we just stepped into a refrigerated room."

Da Souza turned to us and smiled. "Technically," she said, "you have."

We looked past her and gazed into the chamber.

I gasped. Triangular like the last chamber, it stretched away into the distance for as far as the eye could see: the perspective was dizzying, almost vertiginous. I had never had this long a view constricted by walls—normally such vistas were panoramic and open—and the effect on the senses was unsettling, oddly claustrophobic.

"It's almost three kilometres in length," Da Souza said in an appropriately hushed voice.

"But what is it?" Matt said.

We began walking, and our sudden encroachment into the chamber re-emphasized how tiny we were by comparison: we were like ants in a cathedral.

An aisle ran the length of the chamber, dwindling to a distant vanishing point, and on either side were ranged what looked like catafalques: metal oval pods, for want of a better word, on top of which lay the recumbent effigies of short, incredibly grotesque aliens.

"There must be thousands of them," I said.

"We have calculated there are a just over half a million," Da Souza said.

Maddie approached the nearest catafalque. Hand in hand, Hannah and I joined her.

The pod and the alien appeared to be cast from the same dark, metallic substance, which seemed to be running with oil. The fluid, reflective surface gave the figure a semblance of life at odds with its stasis.

It was humanoid, but only just: short and squat, vaguely reptilian, though its face was squashed and an ugly array of tusks sprouted from a slit-like aperture which presumably was its mouth.

Hawk said, "Is it a statue? Or a tomb?"

Da Souza gazed down at the alien. "We don't know if it's solid or not, or whether it is or was alive . . . All we know is that they're as old as the chamber itself." She shrugged. "We wanted to open the chamber to the public, but we were wary of how the Ashentay might react—given their reluctance to allow Dr Petronious down here."

"And?" Matt asked.

"And they had no objections. We met with the Elders just last week and they said, cryptically, that they knew that no ill-fortune would come to anyone who ventured down here."

"What the hell did they mean by that?" Hawk asked.

Da Souza smiled. "You know the Ashentay as well as I do, Mr Hawksworth. Their pronouncements are merely translations from their own tongue, and much of the subtler shades of meaning are often lost."

Maddie reached out and touched the high, arched ribcage of the alien figure. Her eyes widened. I lay a hand on the figure's shoulder. It was warm, like the silver spears I had touched yesterday.

"And we can't explain the heat, either," Da Souza said. "By every reckoning, the pods and the figures should be cold to the touch."

I recalled Kee's shivery pronouncement yesterday as to the creepiness of the chambers. I wondered what she would make of this one.

Hawk moved back to the centre of the aisle and gazed along its length. "It reminds me of an army," he said. "A sleeping army. With its war vehicles in the next chamber . . . "

"And the silver spears?" I said.

He shrugged. "Its weapons?"

I laughed. "You're letting your imagination get the best of you, Hawk."

Maddie said, "Almost a million years . . . they've been sleeping here for a million years!"

"Always assuming," Matt said, "they're sleeping. This puts me in mind more of a . . . museum, or a mausoleum. A place of worship, perhaps, a monument to their fallen dead."

"The sad fact is," Da Souza said, "that we'll probably never know." She moved towards the triangular entrance, and we took one last look around the extraterrestrial chamber before joining her.

I realised, as we made our way back through the chambers to the stairway, that on my arrival here I had been a little drunk: now I was stone-cold sober.

As we climbed, the warmth of the rainforest seemed to embrace us. We passed from the stairwell and Da Souza locked the solid metal door behind us. We emerged into the muted roar of the waterfall and passed beneath it, the rushing wall of water to our left shining a phosphorescent silver in the ring-light.

At last we came to the wooden walkway and climbed to our villa. As we reached the top, Da Souza paused and stared into the forest.

We came to a halt behind her, alerted by something in her frozen posture.

"What?" Hannah whispered.

I stared into the shady forest, imagining a thousand pairs of Ashentay eyes staring back at me.

In a soft voice our guide said, "We've noticed increased activity in the Ashentay of late. The local population has swelled; they've come from kilometres around . . . It seems as if, for some reason, they are massing here."

She waved goodnight and, with her words still ringing in our ears, we made our way back to the villa in silence.

NINE

WHEN KEE RETURNED TO THE ROOM she was sharing with Hawk, I looked in on Ella. She was fast asleep on her back, arms splayed, blonde hair dishevelled. I stood on the threshold of the room for a few minutes, staring at my daughter in the ring-light. There are some sights just too ineffable to label with the appropriate emotion: I'll be lazy and simply say that I felt a sudden upwelling of love for Ella.

I slept well that night and awoke only once to find Hannah pressed to my back, her lips wet on my shoulder. I smiled to myself and stared at the silver light slanting through the wall of the room, then slept again.

I was awoken abruptly just before dawn. I sat up and swung myself out of bed, an image dissolving as I came to my senses. I tried to recall the dream, the warning . . .

"Ella!" I cried out.

Hannah was awake beside me. "David?"

I stood, tugging on my shorts. "Ella . . ." I said again, more to myself this time.

Hannah reached out and placed a calming hand on my arm. "What is it . . . ?"

"I . . . A dream. I had a dream." I closed my eyes, confused. "Ella was in danger."

I hurried from the room, Hannah close behind me.

I came to Ella's room and pulled open the door. My heart jumped as I saw the empty bed. I stepped into the room, gripped by a terrible fear. "Ella?"

I stared around wildly, Hannah beside me now, shock vivid on her face.

Terrible scenarios played themselves out in my fevered mind: we were high up, next to a thousand-metre drop . . . the was a pool on the roof . . . the forest began just metres away, and who knew what dangers lurked there . . .

Crazed with fear, I pushed past Hannah and hurried from the villa, yelling, "Ella!" at the top of my lungs. "Ella!"

I stood on the patio, whirling like a madman, looking everywhere but seeing nothing.

The others were hurrying from their rooms, pulling on clothing as they came, identical expressions of worry making their features oddly uniform.

"David?"

"Ella's gone! She's not in her room. She was there last night—I looked in. She's gone!"

I tried to keep the fear at bay, but I could not help but feel a harrowing, pre-emptive grief for Ella—out of all proportion to what might have happened—and at the same time an echo of the grief I had experienced in the aftermath of losing Carrie all those years ago.

Hannah was clutching me, tearful now. Matt gripped my arm. "It's okay, David. We'll find her, okay?"

Kee hurried from the villa, staring at me. She took my hand. "This way, David."

I shook my hand. "What?" I felt a sudden surge of hope, followed by the rational thought: how on earth could Kee know the whereabouts of my daughter?

Maddie said, "Do you know where Ella is, Kee?"

The alien girl turned a serious face to Maddie and said, "Ella is making her way to the third chamber."

My senses swam. I laughed, unable to take in the logic of her words.

"How do you know?" Hannah said, admirably calm.

"We . . . my people . . . we know," was Kee's reply.

Maddie was already pulling out her com. "I'll contact Da Souza. She has the key—"

She fell silent, stopped by the logic of her words. She stared at me, and did not need to say: *but how could Ella gain access to the chamber . . . ?*

Kee was pulling me towards the steps that led into the forest. "This way. Ella went this way."

Unable to bring myself to trust Kee's certainty, and beset by fears for Ella's welfare, I could feel only anger welling in my chest. Hannah took my hand as Kee raced ahead, a dryad figure as she paused in the fringe of the foliage and looked back, gesturing us to hurry.

We caught up with her and plunged into the forest, Matt and Maddie close behind us. I found myself asking where Hawk was, and without stopping Kee replied, "Hawk has gone to get his ship."

I could only laugh at this, almost hysterically. "His ship?" I said.

But Kee was accelerating with every step and failed to hear my question, or perhaps chose to ignore it.

It came to me then that we were heading up the incline, and not down as we should have been doing if we wished to enter the alien chambers.

Seconds later my unvoiced query was answered. We came to the clearing where the standing stone stood. Or, rather, where the standing stone no longer stood.

I became aware of two things simultaneously: that the great monolith was on its side, and that in the forest all around were the Ashentay, watching us.

Only then did I see the shadow in the ground where the stone had stood; then my eyes adjusted in the dappled half-light of the Ring and I could see that the shadow was a hole in the ground. I approached it and made out small steps, leading down.

Kee was already slipping into the mouth of the hole, beckoning me. I followed, stumbling as I tried to negotiate the steps: they were tiny, made for feet smaller than mine, and I braced myself against the earth for support. I heard Hannah behind me. I assumed Matt and Maddie were bringing up the rear; I recall wanting them here, with me; needing them.

There was no natural light down here, but Kee had thought of that. She was holding something above her head, a stick that gave off a dull glow, enough to make out her slight figure and the walls to either side.

The tunnel took a steep dive, and it was all I could do to grip the stone walls and stop myself from tumbling.

I have no idea whether I was attempting to explain events with some rational narrative at the time; I think I was too dazed and afraid to impose logic on the illogicality that was happening. All I wanted was to have Ella in my arms again. All else: *why* she had taken off like this, *what* the Ashentay and Kee had to do with it . . . all this was secondary and of little concern beside my immediate worry.

Behind me, Matt said, "Kee, why has Hawk gone for the ship?"

Without pausing, Kee said over her shoulder. "Because it is said that he must. We all have our parts in the . . . " and she said a word I didn't recognise, an Ashentay word, obviously, which sounded like *shalan* . . . "and Hawk must do his duty."

And my part? I wondered. Had my part been merely to ensure that my daughter came to Tamara Falls?

Seconds later Kee halted, and I almost fetched up against her. She pushed something, and a section of the wall before her swung forward. We were in the first alien chamber, the area of silver spears, and as we tumbled from the confines of the tunnel, the movement-sensitive lighting flickered on, temporarily dazzling us.

I stumbled through the spears, calling, "Ella!"

Hannah caught up with me, gripping my hand. I returned the pressure, aware that I did not want to be alone during the events that were destined to play themselves out in the minutes and hours that followed.

Kee was racing ahead, down the aisle between the spears towards the second chamber. We gave chase, passing through the cavern of racked starships in what seemed like seconds before arriving, breathless, at the flimsy door marked "Off Limits".

It stood ajar. Kee stepped through the narrow gap without having to open it further. I wrenched it wide with an angry gesture and ran into the vast third chamber.

And stopped.

Much had changed since we'd visited the chamber hours earlier. For one thing, the air was warm, charged with something that had the tang of ozone, or electricity—and an eerie humming filled the cavern.

One hundred metres ahead of us, in the centre of the aisle, something vast and cylindrical, carved with alien hieroglyphs, was rising slowly from the floor, its oiled metal exterior identical to that of the pods and figures on either side.

And before it, like a supplicant at an altar, was Ella.

I stood transfixed, unable to move. The cylinder rose, unscrewing itself from the floor, something malign about the speed of its ascent. Or perhaps I ascribed its malignancy only later, when I understood fully what was happening.

The cylinder stopped suddenly, and the charged hum that filled the air rose in pitch.

I found that I could move again, and hurried forward. Ella was only a hundred metres away, but I seemed unable to close the gap between us.

Something glowed in the flank of the cylinder facing my daughter. She was holding something, I saw now: the cone from the necklace. As I watched, frozen, she stepped forward, raised the cone and approached the glowing face of the cylinder.

I called out to stop her doing what she was about to do—but something stopped my cry.

A familiar green glow suffused the chamber. I heard Hannah and Maddie gasp in alarm. I stared.

The attenuated spectre of the Yall floated before us, staring at us. As we backed away, it spoke.

"Do not prevent your daughter from doing this. It must happen. There is danger, but it is *shalan*." Its words were oddly loud, in that they filled the chamber, but at the same time were gentle, almost quiet. "*Shalan*: that which is meant to be, an evil that must be faced, and then defeated. Please, do not fear. All will be well."

"What . . . " I managed at last. "What the hell is going on?"

But all the pacific, floating ghost would say was, "It is *shalan*." It turned towards Ella as she lifted the cone and inserted it into the face of the cylinder.

She stepped back suddenly, as if she had received a jolt of electricity.

And then the cylinder split open and something from Hell stepped forth.

The creature resembled the figures on the pods, but this one was ineluctably organic: it appeared slick with fluid, like a machine-part stored in grease for years, and its metallic blue carapace scintillated in the light of the cavern. It stepped forward, hunched, a monster, part-insect, part-reptile, and opened its dripping mandibles.

I backed away, despite the fear for my daughter, and deep within me I felt a terrible recapitulation of the cowardice which, years ago, had prevented me from saving Carrie.

Ella stood frozen before the creature, tiny by comparison.

The creature turned its great prognathus head, taking in the chamber, then settling its gaze on our tiny, terrified tableau: Hannah and myself, Matt and Maddie, and the spectre of the Yall.

It stepped forward again, almost tumbling Ella in the process, its great clawed feet clanking on the aisle. Ella stared up, petrified.

The apparition of the Yall moved from us, down the aisle, and confronted the creature.

The Yall spoke, and the creature replied, and seconds later their dialogue was rendered intelligible to us.

"You awake at last," said the Yall.

"A million years. A short sleep, for the likes of the Skeath."

"You awake, soon to be cast into the depths for ever."

The creature opened its nightmare jaws and gave a mechanical, grating roar, conveying its contempt. Then, "You were a worthy enemy, Yall. You fought us well, even if you were always destined to lose."

"We did not lose. We . . . we changed."

The beast clanked forward, dripping fluid, and as the drops hit the aisle, they sizzled. "Changed? Changed into the virtual ghosts I see before me?"

"Changed into a people which will defeat the Skeath once again."

"Again?" the monster roared. "You did not defeat my kind a million years ago. We . . . we merely made a tactical retreat, here, to bide our time, to outlive millennia, until we rose again . . . "

The Yall gestured, peaceably. "Believe whatever delusion makes you content, Skeath. You will soon learn the truth."

"The truth is that my kind are risen!" the creature thundered. "The truth is that we will dominate the galaxy, as we did once, before you drove us back."

And as it spoke, I heard a series of what sounded like detonations echo around the chamber. I looked around and saw, to my horror, that the pods that lined the aisle were snapping open, and that the creatures within, smaller versions of their leader, were emerging.

What had Da Souza said, that there were more than half a million of these pods within the chamber?

The Yall, apparently unperturbed by this turn of events, said, "My people have waited a long time for this encounter. It was inevitable, and desirable, that it should happen—to allow me to pass judgement on the Skeath: that you should be banished from this place and dispatched to a realm from which you will never be able to terrorise the innocent again, where you will be no threat to the peaceable peoples of the galaxy."

"Words!" cried the Skeath. With an outswept arm it gestured to its risen army. "Annihilate them!"

And before I could even begin to feel fear, another change took hold within the chamber. A great roar filled the air. At first I thought the waterfall had found its way down here—and then chamber was filled with light, an effulgent, golden light, and I felt elated.

We were like flies in amber, tiny creatures transfixed, then, in a medium like sunlight made solid, and I knew precisely what had happened.

Seconds later a small starship appeared to our right, sending pods and the alien army skittling as it did so. A hatch fell open, revealing the lighted interior of Hawk's cruiser.

I turned to the Skeath and the Yall, and the latter gestured towards the ship. "Go, you have played your part. Go quickly."

I ran forward, towards the monster, and plucked Ella from its shadow. Kee was already sprinting through the golden glow towards the cruiser, followed by Matt and Maddie. Gripping Hannah's hand and clutching Ella to me, we raced towards the ship. On either side the alien army raised its weapons.

We staggered up the ramp and into the sanctuary of the ship. I ran through to the flight-deck, where Hawk was strapped into his sling, wires and cables connecting him to the smartcore.

Seconds later the ship vibrated, its engines powering up.

I held Hannah and Ella and stared through the viewscreen as the Skeath and its army brought their weapons to bear on the apparition of the Yall—

"Hold on!" Hawk yelled.

I cried out as the Skeath poured fire upon the Yall . . .

And then we were no longer in the chamber, no longer underground. We had left the golden column and were speeding through bright blue sky above Tamara Falls.

Hawk banked the ship and held it steady perhaps a kilometre from where the shaft of the column thrust from the Falls. We crowded around the viewscreen, staring at the wonder before us, the dazzling trunk of light identical to the Golden Column one hundred kilometres to the north.

And I knew then what the Yall had commanded Hawk to do.

Kee was explaining to Matt and Maddie. "The Yall came to Hawk, too," she said in a quiet voice, "and told him to take this ship and fly it into the Golden Column, with the exit point at the Falls preset, so creating *this* column."

"And now?" Maddie asked.

Kee smiled. "Now watch," she said, gesturing towards the viewscreen.

We turned our attention to the golden column ascending from the Falls, and seconds later—like an optical illusion which leaves the observer baffled and incredulous—it vanished.

Hawk brought his ship down on the landing pad above the villa, and Kee led the way through the jungle to a hillock overlooking the waterfall. From this vantage point we could see across the broad swathe of water to the far bank—and the vast, circular pit whose darkness contrasted with the blue of the river and the vivid green of the forest. It was as if a great cheese-screw had been inserted into the land, turned and withdrawn, taking out a column of bedrock and all it contained and leaving a perfectly circular hole in its stead.

Already, fascinated tourists were making their way up the walkways and crossing the Falls to get closer to the pit. One or two small planes circled in the clear blue sky, their pilots no doubt incredulous at the inexplicable phenomenon far below.

"It's gone, Daddy," Ella said, voicing our collective amazement.

"What did the Yall say?" Maddie asked. "That the Skeath should be dispatched to a realm from which they would never be able to terrorise the innocent again . . . "

"I wonder where that might be?" Hawk said.

"Imagine the media interest in this," I said. "I just hope we can keep our involvement a secret."

Kee looked at me, seriously. "David, do not worry about that. My people, the Elders, will explain the threat of the Skeath to the authorities, and they will not mention your part in their banishment."

As we turned from the river and made our way back through the rainforest, I realised that although much had been explained by the events of the last hour, there were many questions yet to be answered.

Not that I cared . . .

I carried Ella on my back, joyous at her safe return.

TEN

THREE DAYS LATER we were lounging beside the pool in the dappled sunlight filtering through the shola trees. Maddie emerged from the villa with a tray of drinks, followed by Hawk. Hannah sat up and removed her sunglasses, smiling across to where Ella was splashing in the pool.

Kee sat to one side, staring into the forest. She had been quiet since the day of the encounter with the Skeath, and as if in tacit agreement we had refrained from pressing her with questions relating to her involvement in the affair.

Matt wandered from the villa like a man in a daze. He was staring down at a softscreen, eyes wide as he read.

He dropped into a lounger beside mine and passed me the screen. "Well," he announced. "News just in from Kallash, Antares . . . The entrepreneur and patron of the arts Dr Petronious . . . he's been found dead in his penthouse suite in the capital. Took his own life, according to the report."

I stared at the moving picture of Petronious opening some cultural event on his planet, filmed just days before his suicide. The report contained no more than Matt had already precised.

"I hope that doesn't affect his purchase of your art, Matt," Hannah said.

"All that was completed weeks ago. His Foundation will continue with the exhibitions." He looked up. "I've been thinking about the money, anyway—even before all this blew up. I was thinking of donating most of it to some scheme to assist novice artists. I couldn't keep what he paid me, after what happened."

Kee stood up quickly and I became aware of a sudden charge in the air, as at the approach of a thunderstorm... which was absurd: the sun shone unremittingly; the temperature was in the high twenties.

We all looked around, aware at the same time of movement in the forest that enclosed the pool area on three sides. I caught glimpses of fleet bodies there, glimpsed the flash of observant eyes.

"Attention!" Kee sang out, rigid now and staring into the air between us.

Seconds later the air shimmered, and a faint figure took shape in the sunlight. The Yall apparition floated, regarding us.

My heart began a laboured pounding. I wanted to gauge the reaction of my friends, but I couldn't tear my gaze from the spectre.

"This will be the last time we will come to you, my friends," the Yall began. "The galaxy has the Golden Columns, but more importantly, the galaxy is no longer threatened by the evil of the Skeath. I—we—thank you for your assistance once again."

Matt managed a question, "You knew this... the awakening of the Skeath... would occur one day?"

"We knew of the danger of its happening, yes. For millennia after what we thought was our final battle with the Skeath, we searched for their remnants. My people, the Yall, became withdrawn. We left behind us the way of technology; we inhabited planets across the galaxy, this one included, and took to the forests. We adapted ourselves genetically to suit conditions here: over time we changed, devolved, you could say. Only a thousand years ago was the retreat of the Skeath discovered on Chalcedony.

"Then we began the search for the key that would bring the army back to terrible life... But only when the Antarian, Dr Petronious, travelled here with the cone, did the Ashentay Elders understand."

Matt said, "Petronious was a Skeath?"

The apparition gestured. "He was Antarian, but he knew the legend of the Skeath, and on behalf of his government he worked to bring the Skeath battalions from hibernation and, perhaps he dreamed of one day using their might on behalf of his planet. Little did he understand their evil; that they would fight for no one but themselves."

I said, "And where are they now, the Skeath battalions?"

"We are not a violent people. We did not punish the Skeath with death. We merely banished them, without their ships or weapons, to a distant world where they will bother no one ever again. And the location of that planet shall remain a secret."

I noticed Kee then. She was kneeling before the spectral Yall, her head bowed as if in supplication, and something the ghost had said returned to me.

"You said . . . you said that your people inhabited planets across the galaxy, including this one, and that you devolved . . . "

"Devolved", said the figure, "is a cruel word. Perhaps the correct word would be *evolved*."

Maddie said, "You became . . . ?"

And before us, the apparition of the Yall began slowly to change. The attenuated green reptilian form lost its height, its jade colouration: it became, gradually, a slight, golden figure, lithe and athletic . . . and familiar.

The apparition said, "The Ashentay, my friends, are the descendants of the Yall."

My head spinning, I said, "And you?"

I knew the answer, of course, before the spectre voiced the words.

"I . . . or rather the figure you see before you . . . am nothing more than a representation of the aggregate unconscious of the Ashentay people."

And with these words the figure began to fade, and at the same time I became aware of movement in the forest around us as the Ashentay watchers departed, retreating with the fluid rapidity of their kind into the cool shadows of the forest.

The figure disappeared and I searched for the last vestiges of it above the patio; I convinced myself that I could see its face, smiling at me, but that might only have been my wishful thinking.

Ella jumped from the pool and ran into Hannah's arms. A silence enveloped us as we took in the import of what the Yall had told us.

Hawk pulled Kee to him and held her, tight.

I looked around at my friends, at Matt and Maddie, holding hands, at Hawk and Kee—two very different souls, now one—and at my wife and daughter.

And I felt exalted.

Matt broke the spell. He raised his glass and in a hushed, reverential tone, proposed a toast.

"To the Yall," he said.

"To the Yall . . . " we replied.

The Starship Quartet
by Eric Brown

—

Starship Summer

—

Starship Fall

—

Starship Winter

—

Starship Spring

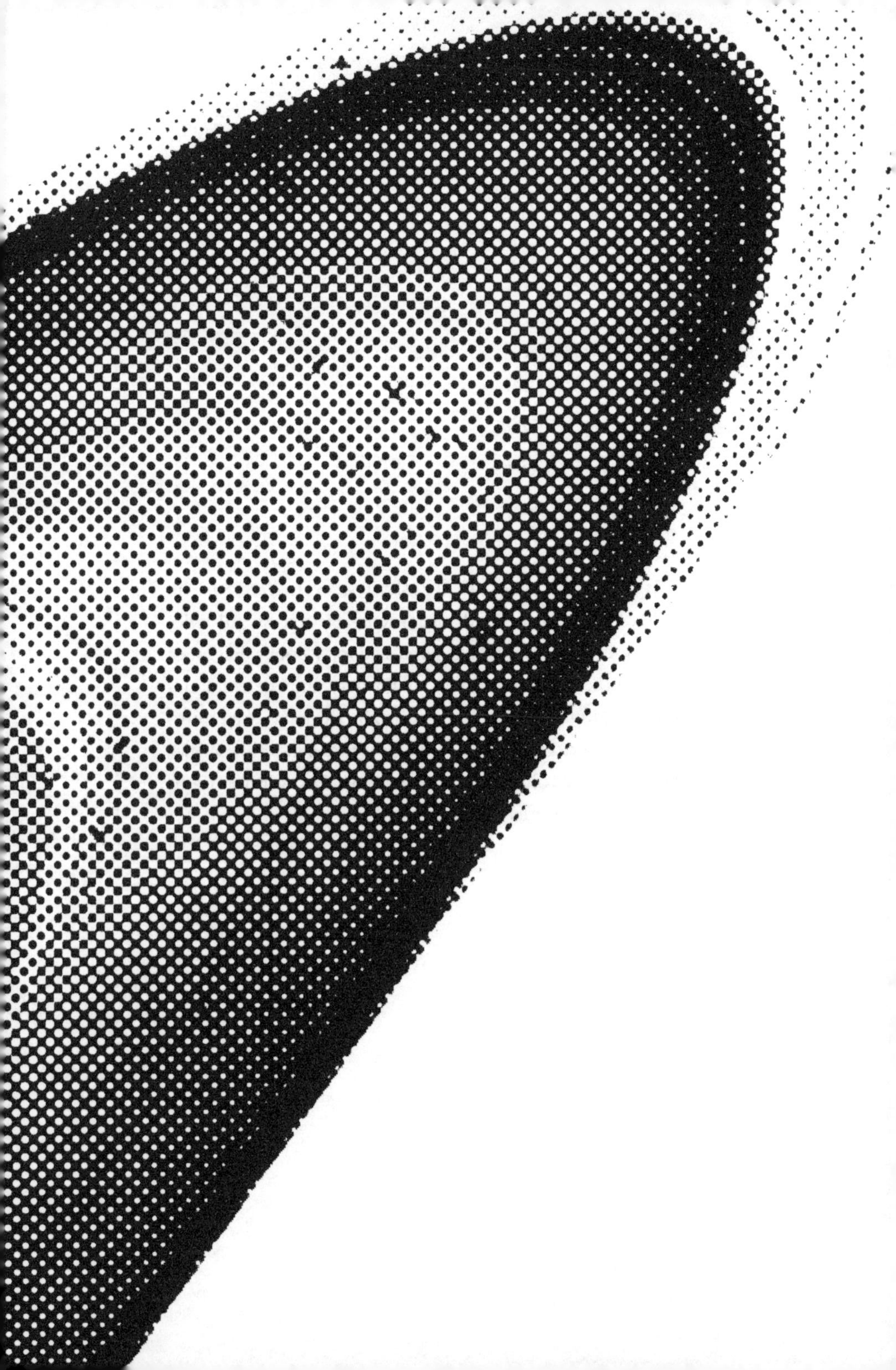

ERIC BROWN sold his first short story to *Interzone* in 1986. He has won the British Science Fiction Award twice for his short stories and has published forty books. His latest include the novel *The Kings of Eternity* and the children's book *A Monster Ate My Marmite*. His work has been translated into sixteen languages, and he writes a monthly science fiction review column for the *Guardian*. His website can be found at: www.ericbrownsf.co.uk